THE BRIDGE ON THE RIVER KWAI

PIERRE BOULLE

The Bridge on the River Kwai

Translated from the French by *Xan Fielding*

FONTANA / Collins

LE PONT DE LA RIVIÈRE KWAI

Copyright 1952 by René Julliard
First published 1954 by Secker & Warburg
First issued in Fontana Books 1956
Twenty-ninth impression April 1988

Printed and bound in Great Britain by
William Collins Sons & Co. Ltd, Glasgow

No, it was not funny; it was rather pathetic; he was so representative of all the past victims of the Great Joke. But it is by folly alone that the world moves, and so it is a respectable thing upon the whole. And besides he was what one would call a good man.

JOSEPH CONRAD

PART ONE

I

The insuperable gap between East and West that exists in
some eyes is perhaps nothing more than an optical illusion.
Perhaps it is only the conventional way of expressing a
popular opinion based on insufficient evidence and mas-
querading as a universally recognised statement of fact, for
which there is no justification at all, not even the plea that
it contains an element of truth. During the last war 'saving
face' was perhaps as vitally important to the British as it
was to the Japanese. Perhaps it dictated the behaviour of
the former, without their being aware of it, as forcibly and
as fatally as it did that of the latter, and no doubt that of
every other race in the world. Perhaps the conduct of each
of the two enemies, superficially so dissimilar, was in fact
simply a different though equally meaningless manifestation
of the same spiritual reality. Perhaps the mentality of the
Japanese colonel, Saito, was essentially the same as that of
his prisoner, Colonel Nicholson.

These were the questions which occupied Major Clipton's
thoughts. He too was a prisoner, like the five hundred other
wretches herded by the Japanese into the camp on the
River Kwai, like the sixty thousand English, Australians,
Dutch and Americans assembled in several groups in one of
the most uncivilised corners of the earth, the jungle of
Burma and Siam, in order to build a railway linking the Bay
of Bengal to Bangkok and Singapore. Clipton occasionally
answered these questions in the affirmative, realising, however, that this point of view was in the nature of a paradox;
to acquire it one had to disregard all superficial appearances.
Above all, one had to assume that the beatings-up, the butt-

end blows and even worse forms of brutality through which the Japanese mentality made itself felt were all as meaningless as the show of ponderous dignity which was Colonel Nicholson's favourite weapon, wielded as a mark of British superiority. But Clipton willingly gave way to this assumption each time his C.O.'s behaviour enraged him to such an extent that the only consolation he could find was in a whole-hearted objective examination of primary causes.

He invariably came to the conclusion that the combination of individual characteristics which contributed to Colonel Nicholson's personality (sense of duty, observance of ritual, obsession with discipline and love of the job well done were all jumbled together in this worthy human repository) could not be better described than by the single word: snobbery. During these periods of feverish investigation he regarded him as a snob, a perfect example of the military snob, which has gradually emerged after a lengthy process of development dating from the Stone Age, the preservation of the species being guaranteed by tradition.

Clipton, however, was by nature objective and had the rare gift of being able to examine a problem from every angle. The conclusion he had reached having somewhat calmed the brainstorm which certain aspects of the Colonel's behaviour caused him, he would suddenly feel well disposed and recognise, almost with affection, the excellence of the C.O.'s qualities. If these were typically snobbish, he reasoned, then the argument need be carried only one stage further for the noblest sentiments to be likewise classified as such, until even a mother's love would eventually come to be regarded as the most blatant sign of snobbery imaginable.

In the past, Colonel Nicholson's high regard for discipline has been a byword in various parts of Asia and Africa. In 1942 it was once again in evidence, at Singapore, during the disaster which followed the invasion of Malaya.

When orders came through from Headquarters to cease fire, a group of young officers in his battalion had planned to make their way down to the coast, get hold of a boat and set sail for the Dutch East Indies. Although admiring their zeal and courage, Colonel Nicholson had hindered their scheme with every means at his disposal.

To begin with, he had tried to win them over by pointing out that this venture was a direct contravention of the instructions he had received. Since the Commander-in-Chief had signed the surrender for the whole of Malaya, not one of His Majesty's subjects could escape without committing an act of disobedience. As far as he could see, there was only one line of conduct possible: to stay put until a senior Japanese officer turned up to accept the surrender of himself and his unit and of the hundreds of stragglers who had managed to escape the massacre of the last few weeks.

'A fine example it would be for the men,' he had exclaimed, 'if their officers failed in their duty!'

His argument had been rendered additionally forceful by the piercing look of resolution which he always assumed in moments of crisis. His eyes were the colour of the Indian Ocean on a calm day; and his features, which were always in repose, were the clear reflection of a guiltless conscience. His fair, reddish moustache was the moustache of an unruffled hero; and his ruddy complexion was evidence of a sound heart regulating a smooth, easy circulation perfect in its efficiency. Clipton, who had served under him throughout the campaign, never ceased to wonder at this living example of 'the Indian Army officer,' a type which he had always considered legendary, but whose reality was now proclaimed so loudly every day that it invariably caused him these alternating bouts of anger and affection.

Clipton had pleaded the young officer's case. He approved of it and said so. Colonel Nicholson had taken him to task and declared himself painfully surprised to see a middle-aged man in a highly responsible position sharing the wild aspirations of a lot of hot-headed youngsters and encouraging the sort of thoughtless escapade that can cause nothing but harm.

Having explained the reason for his attitude, he had issued strict and definite orders. All officers, N.C.O.s and men were to stay put until the Japanese arrived. Their surrender was not of their own choice; none of them, therefore, should feel in any way humiliated. He, and he alone, would shoulder the responsibility on behalf of the whole battalion.

Most of the officers had given in to him; for his power of persuasion was considerable, and his authority immense, while his unquestionable personal courage made it impossible to attribute his conduct to any motive except sense of duty. Some of them had disobeyed orders and disappeared into the jungle. Colonel Nicholson had been genuinely grieved by their behaviour. He had posted them as deserters, and with growing impatience had waited for the Japanese to appear.

In preparation for their arrival, he had worked out in his head a ceremony which would bear the stamp of quiet dignity. After considerable thought he had decided, as a symbolic act of submission, to hand over the revolver which he wore on his hip to the enemy colonel in charge of the surrender. He had rehearsed the gesture several times and had made certain of being able to take the holster off in one easy movement. He had put on his best uniform and seen that his men tidied themselves up. Then he had ordered them to fall in and pile arms and had inspected them in person.

The first to make contact were some private soldiers who could not speak a word of any civilised language. Colonel Nicholson had not budged. Then a N.C.O. had driven up in a truck and motioned the British to load their arms on to the vehicle. The Colonel had forbidden his men to move. He had demanded to see a senior officer. There was no officer, either senior or junior, and the Japanese did not understand his request. They had turned nasty. The soldiers had assumed a threatening attitude, while the N.C.O. broke out into shrill screams and pointed at the rifles. The Colonel had ordered his men to stay put and not move. Submachine-guns had been pointed at them, while the Colonel was unceremoniously pushed around. He had kept his temper and repeated his demand. The British began to look rather worried and Clipton was wondering if the C.O. intended to get them all massacred out of loyalty to his principles and for the sake of form, when a car full of Japanese officers at last appeared. One of them wore the badges of rank of a major. *Faute de mieux*, Colonel Nicholson decided to surrender to him. He called his unit to attention. He himself saluted in exemplary fashion, and taking his holster off his belt, presented it with a flourish.

Faced with this gift, the astonished major first stepped back in alarm; then he appeared extremely embarrassed; finally he became convulsed by a long burst of savage laughter in which he was soon joined by his fellow-officers. Colonel Nicholson simply shrugged his shoulders and assumed a haughty expression: none the less he gave his men the order to load their rifles on to the truck.

During the time that he had spent in the prison camp near Singapore, Colonel Nicholson had made a point of observing a strict Anglo-Saxon code of behaviour in face of the enemy's disorderly conduct. Clipton, who had been with him all the time, was not sure even at that early date whether to bless him or curse him.

As a result of the orders he had issued, orders which confirmed and amplified the Japanese instructions, the men in his unit behaved well and fared badly. Bully-beef and other miscellaneous supplies, which the prisoners from other units sometimes managed to 'win' in the blitzed outskirts of Singapore in spite of, and often in connivance with, the sentries, were a welcome supplement to the meagre rations. But this sort of looting was not permitted on any account by Colonel Nicholson. He made his officers give lectures condemning such behaviour as undignified and pointing out that the only way for the British soldier to command the respect of his temporary masters was to set them an example of irreproachable conduct. He saw to it that this order was obeyed by carrying out regular inspections, which were even more thorough than the sentries'!

These lectures on the standard of behaviour which every soldier was supposed to keep up when serving overseas were not the only fatigues which he imposed on his battalion. During that period the unit was by no means overwhelmed with work, since the Japanese had organised no labour to speak of in the outskirts of Singapore. Convinced that idleness was prejudicial to the spirit of the regiment, and frightened at the prospect of a drop in morale, the Colonel had drawn up a full programme for every off-duty hour. He made his officers read out and explain to the men whole sections of *King's Regulations*, after which he examined them and issued rewards in the shape of certificates bearing his signature. Discipline, of course, was not the least important subject in this curriculum. At regular intervals it was brought to the notice of all ranks that correct saluting was compulsory, even in a prison compound. Consequently the privates, who were also obliged to salute every Japanese irrespective of his rank, ran a double risk every time they neglected instructions: on the other hand, they risked the kicks and blows of the sentries; on the other, a dressing down from the Colonel and some punishment imposed by him, such as having to stand to attention for several hours during recreation periods.

The fact that such Spartan discipline had been generally accepted by the men, and that they had voluntarily submitted to an authority which was no longer backed up by the powers-that-be, but was only wielded by an individual at the mercy of the same abuses and ill-treatment as themselves, was a frequent source of amazement to Clipton. He often wondered whether such obedience should be attributed to the personal respect which the Colonel commanded or to the privileges which they enjoyed thanks to him; for no one could deny that his intransigent attitude was successful, even with the Japanese. His chief weapons, when dealing with them, were his insistence on a proper code of conduct, his tenacity, his ability to keep harping on one particular point until he obtained satisfaction, and the *Manual of Military Law* containing the Hague Convention which he calmly waved in the Japs' faces each time a breach of international law was committed. His personal courage and complete disregard for the blows he received were also no doubt largely responsible for the high regard in which he was held. On several occasions, when the Japanese had exceeded the recognised rights due to a victorious army, he had done more than protest. He had personally intervened. He had once been badly beaten up by a particularly brutal guard who had issued an order contrary to international law. He had eventually scored his point, and his assailant had been punished. He had then proceeded to issue his own version of the order, which was far harsher than anything the Japanese could devise.

'The main thing,' he explained, when Clipton suggested that in the circumstances he might exercise a little leniency, 'the main thing is to make the lads feel they're still being commanded by us and not by these baboons. As long as they cling to this idea, they'll be soldiers, not slaves.'

Clipton, who could see both sides of the question, had to admit there was something to be said for this and realised that the Colonel's action was prompted, as usual, by his sterling qualities.

II

The prisoners now recalled those months they had spent in the Singapore camp as a period of palmy days, and sighed with regret when they compared it with their present plight in this uncivilised corner of Siam. They had reached their destination after an endless train journey right across Malaya, followed by an exhausting march in the course of which they had grown so weak from exposure and malnutrition that bit by bit they had jettisoned the heaviest and most valuable items of their wretched equipment, without any hope of ever getting them back. The rumours about the railway which they were going to build did not cheer them up at all.

Colonel Nicholson and his unit had been moved a little later than the others, and the work was already under way by the time they reached Siam. After the hardships of their cross-country march, their first encounter with the new Japanese authorities had been far from encouraging. At Singapore they had been up against soldiers who, after the

initial frenzy of victory, and apart from a few isolated out-
breaks of primitive brutality, had proved to be not much
more oppressive than any Western army of occupation
would have been. The officers in charge of the Allied prisoners on the railway were evidently quite a different proposition. From the very start they had acted like savage chain-
gang warders and were liable to turn at a moment's notice
into sadistic executioners.

Colonel Nicholson and the remainder of his battalion,
which he still prided himself on commanding, had at first
to be transferred to a vast reception centre serving as a
transit camp for all the convoys along this route, part of
which, however, was already in use as permanent quarters.
They had stayed there only a short time, but long enough to
realise what they were in for and how they would live until
the job was finished. The poor devils were put to work like
beasts of burden. Each of them had to complete a task which
was not perhaps beyond the strength of a man in good
condition and on an adequate diet; for the pitiful, emaciated
creatures that they had become in less than one month, it
was a job that kept them busy from dawn till dusk and
sometimes half the night. They were worn out and demoral-
ised by the curses and blows which the guards rained
down on them at the slightest sign of faltering, and haunted
by the fear of even worse punishment to come. Clipton had
been appalled by their physical condition. Malaria, dysentery, beri-beri and jungle sores were rife, and the camp
M.O. had told him there might be far more serious epi-
demics, against which he could take no precautions at all.
Not even the most rudimentary medical stores were available.

Colonel Nicholson had frowned without saying a word.
He was not 'in charge' of this camp, and considered himself
almost as a guest there. To the British lieutenant-colonel who
ran it under Japanese orders, he had only once expressed
what he felt; that was when he noticed that all the officers
below the rank of major were doing their share of manual
labour on exactly the same footing as the men, in other
words they were digging and carting like navvies. The

lieutenant-colonel had hung his head. He explained that he had done his best to avoid this humiliation and had given in to brutal compulsion only in order to avoid the reprisals from which everyone would have otherwise suffered. Colonel Nicholson had nodded in a manner that showed he was far from convinced, and had then taken refuge in haughty silence.

They had stayed two days in this reception centre, long enough for the Japanese to issue them with some meagre haversack rations and a triangle of coarse cloth which fastened round the waist with strings, which they referred to as 'working kit'; long enough to see General Yamashita perched on a makeshift platform, with his sword at his hip and pale-grey gloves on his hands, and to listen to him first explaining in faulty English that they had been placed under his command in accordance with the wishes of His Imperial Majesty, and then telling them what was expected of them.

The tirade, which lasted over two hours, had been painful to hear and hurt their national pride just as much as the curses and the blows. He had told them that the Japanese had no quarrel with people like them, who had been led astray by the lies of their government; that they would be decently treated so long as they behaved like 'zentlemen,' that is to say if they contributed with all their heart and with all their strength to the South-East Asia Co-Prosperity Sphere. They should all recognise their obligation to His Imperial Majesty, who was giving them this chance to mend the error of their ways by contributing to the common cause and helping to build the railway. Yamashita had then explained that in the general interest he would have to impose the strictest discipline and would tolerate no disobedience. Laziness and neglect would be treated as crimes. Any attempt to escape would be punished by death. The British officers would be responsible to the Japanese for their men's behaviour and efficiency.

'Sickness will not be considered an excuse,' General Yamashita had added. 'Reasonable work is the best thing in the world for keeping a man physically fit, and dysentery would think twice before attacking anyone who makes a daily effort to do his duty towards the Emperor.'

He had concluded on an optimistic note, which had driven his audience wild with anger.

'Be happy in your work,' he had said, 'that's my motto. Make it your motto as well from now on. Those who live up to it will have nothing to fear from me, nor from the officers of the Japanese Grand Army which is now protecting you.'

Then the units had been dispersed, each one moving off to the sector it had been allotted. Colonel Nicholson and his battalion had made their way to the camp on the River Kwai, which was quite far off, only a few miles from the Burmese border. The commandant was Colonel Saito.

III

Some nasty incidents punctuated the first few days in the Kwai camp, where an uneasy undercurrent of tension was at once noticeable in the atmosphere.

The cause of the initial disturbances was Colonel Saito's proclamation stipulating that all officers were to work side by side with the other ranks and on the same footing. This provoked a polite but firm protest from Colonel Nicholson, who outlined his ideas on the subject candidly and method-ically, adding in conclusion that the task of British officers was to command their men and not wield a pick and shovel.

Saito listened to the whole speech without a sign of im-patience—which the Colonel interpreted as a favourable omen—then dismissed him, saying that he would think the matter over. Colonel Nicholson returned full of confidence to the squalid bamboo hut which he shared with Clipton and two other officers. There he repeated for his own per-sonal satisfaction some of the arguments he had used to convince the Japanese. To him each of them seemed quite conclusive, but the soundest of all in his eyes was this: the total output of a few men unused to manual labour was negligible, while the extra effort that would be made under the supervision of efficient officers was immense. In the interests of the Japanese, therefore, and to ensure that the work was properly done, it was preferable not to deprive the officers of their position of authority, which they would lose if they were detailed to do the same fatigues as the men. He warmed to his subject as he outlined it once again for the benefit of his own officers.

'Well, am I right or wrong?' he asked, turning to Major Hughes. 'You're an industrialist. Do you think we'd get any results on a job like this without a hierarchy of responsible executives?'

As a result of the losses during the tragic campaign, his headquarters staff now consisted of only two officers apart from the M.O. Clipton. He had managed to keep them together ever since Singapore, for he liked to have their opinion and always thought it advisable to put his views before them as a subject for collective discussion before taking any decision. Neither of them was a regular officer. Major Hughes in civilian life was the director of a mining company in Malaya. He had been attached to Colonel Nicholson's battalion and the latter had at once recognised his administrative ability. Captain Reeves in peace time had been a Public Works engineer in India. After joining as a Sapper, he had been separated from his unit during the initial fighting and had been picked up by the Colonel, who had appointed him to his advisory staff. He liked collecting specialists round him. He was no military dunderhead. He was the first to realise that some civilian concerns are occasionally run on methods which the army might do well to adopt, and he never missed an opportunity of adding to his own knowledge. He had an equally high regard for technicians and executives.

'I think you're quite right, sir,' Hughes replied.

'So do I,' said Reeves. 'If you want to build a railway line and a bridge (I believe there's some scheme afoot for a bridge across the river, you can't afford any shoddy, amateur work.'

'I'd forgotten you're a specialist in that sort of thing,' the Colonel mused out loud. 'So you'll understand,' he added, 'why I hope I've driven a little sense into that fellow's thick skull.'

'And besides,' Clipton chipped in, looking closely at his C.O., 'if the common-sense argument doesn't work, there's always the *Manual of Military Law* and the Hague Convention.'

'There's always the Hague Convention,' Colonel Nicholson agreed. 'I'm keeping that up my sleeve for a second interview, if necessary.'

Clipton spoke in this sarcastic, pessimistic tone because he was very doubtful indeed of the value of an appeal to common sense. He had heard various reports on Saito's character at the transit camp where they had halted during their march through the jungle. The Japanese officer, it was said, was sometimes open to reason, when he had not been drinking; but he turned into an utterly vicious brute as soon as he hit the bottle.

Colonel Nicholson had launched his protest on the morning of the first day, which had been set aside for moving the prisoners into the semi-derelict quarters. Saito thought it over, as he had promised. He felt there was something fishy about the whole business, and started to drink in order to clear his brain. He gradually convinced himself that the Colonel had shown intolerable lack of respect in questioning his orders, and his attitude changed imperceptibly from suspicion to cold fury.

Having worked himself up into a paroxysm of rage by sundown, he decided to assert his authority and called everyone out on parade. He too had made up his mind to deliver a speech. From his opening words everyone realised that there were dark clouds gathering over the River Kwai.

'I hate the British . . .'

He had started off with this phrase, which he had then inserted between every other sentence as a sort of punctuation mark. He was fairly fluent in English, having at one time served as military attaché in a British possession, a post which he had been forced to give up because of his chronic drunkenness. His career had petered out into the ignominious position which he now held, a chain-gang warder without a hope of promotion. The hatred he felt for the prisoners was intensified by all the humiliation he had suffered from not having seen any action.

'I hate the British,' Colonel Saito declared. 'You're here, under my personal command, to carry out a job which is necessary for the victory of the Japanese Grand Army. I want to tell you, once and for all, that I won't have my orders questioned in any way. I hate the British. Noncompliance will be punished really severely. Discipline has got to be maintained. If any of you are thinking of putting up a show of resistance, let me remind you that I've got power of life and death over the lot of you. I shan't think twice about exercising that power in order to bring the work with which His Imperial Majesty has entrusted me to a successful conclusion. I hate the British. The death of a few prisoners leaves me cold. The death of the whole lot of you is a mere trifle to a senior officer of the Japanese Grand Army.'

He had climbed on to a table, as General Yamashita had done. Like him, he had seen fit to don a pair of pale-grey gloves and polished riding-boots instead of the canvas shoes which he had worn during the day. His sword, needless to say, hung from his hip, and he kept slapping the hilt, either to lend more weight to his words or to work himself up into the state of rage which he considered suitable to the occasion. He was a grotesque figure. His head wobbled on his shoulders like a puppet's. He was roaring drunk, drunk on European alcohol, on the whisky and brandy left behind at Rangoon and Singapore.

As he listened to the nerve-racking words, Clipton remembered the advice he had once been given by a friend of his who had lived for some time with the Japanese. 'Never forget, when you deal with them, that these people believe in their divine destiny as part of an unquestionable creed.' All the same, he thought, there was no race on earth that did not entertain more or less the same religious belief in itself. So he tried to find another reason for this display of self-satisfaction. To be quite honest, he had to admit that in Saito's speech there were certain basic principles to which the whole world subscribed, East and West alike. In the course of it he was able to recognise and identify the various influences behind the words which spluttered on the lips of this Jap: racial pride, a mystic belief in authority, the dread of not being taken seriously, a strange sort of inferiority complex which gave him a jaundiced, suspicious outlook on life, as though he was in perpetual fear of being laughed at. Saito had lived abroad. He must have seen how the British sometimes made fun of certain aspects of the Japanese character, and how comic the affections of a humourless nation were in the eyes of one to whom humour was second nature. But his uncouth manner of speech and uncontrolled gestures could only be attributed to a legacy of brutish violence. Clipton had felt vaguely uneasy when he heard him talking about discipline, but at the sight of him jumping about like a jack-in-the-box he came to the happy conclusion that there was something to be said for the inhabitants of the Western hemisphere: at least they could take their drink like gentlemen.

With their own men looking on, and with the guards crowding round in threatening attitudes so as to emphasise the commandant's fury, the officers listened in silence. They clenched their fists and deliberately assumed expressions of impassive calm, following the example set by Colonel Nicholson, who had given instructions to meet any hostile demonstration with a show of quiet dignity.

After this preamble designed to stir their imaginations, Saito got down to brass tacks. He became quite calm, almost subdued, and for a moment they thought they were going to hear a little sense.

'Now listen, all of you. You know what sort of job it is that His Imperial Majesty has been good enough to allocate to you British prisoners. We've got to connect the capitals of Siam and Burma so as to enable the Japanese convoys to get across the four hundred miles of jungle in between, and to provide a way through to Bengal for the army which has liberated those two countries from European oppression. Japan needs this railway to continue her victorious advance, to enable her to overrun India and so bring this war to a rapid conclusion. So this work had got to be finished as quickly as possible: in six months. Those are His Imperial Majesty's orders. It's in your interest as well. When the war's over, you'll probably be able to go home under the protection of our army.'

Saito continued in an even calmer tone of voice, as though the alcohol in his blood had all evaporated.

'Now, do you want to know what your specific task is, you men who are in this camp under my command? I'll tell you; that's why I've called you out on parade. You'll only have two short stretches of line to build, to link up with the other section. But your particular responsibility will be the erection of a bridge across the River Kwai that you can see over there. That's your main task and you ought to feel proud of it, for it's the most important job on the whole line. It's quite pleasant work, requiring skilled men and not just navvies. What's more, you'll have the honour of being ranked among the pioneers of the South-East Asia Co-Prosperity Sphere.'

'Just the sort of pep-talk a Westerner might have given,' was Clipton's immediate reaction.

'The work, of course, will be under the technical direction of a qualified engineer, a Japanese engineer. For purposes of discipline, you will be under me and my subordinates. So there'll be no shortage of administration staff. For all these reasons, which I've been good enough to explain, I've given orders for the British officers to work side by side with their men. Things being what they are, I can't have a lot of idle mouths to feed. I hope I shall not have to repeat this order. Otherwise . . .'

Saito relapsed without warning into his initial state of frenzy and started raving like a madman.

'Otherwise I'll have to use force. I hate the British. I'll have you all shot, if necessary, rather than give food to slackers. Sickness will not be considered a reason for exemption. A sick man can always make an effort. I'll build that bridge over the prisoners' dead bodies, if I have to. I hate the British. Work will begin at dawn to-morrow. You will

parade here on the first blast of the whistle. The officers will
fall in as well. They'll form a separate squad on their own,
and they'll be expected to get through the same amount of
work as the rest of you. Tools will be issued and the Japanese engineer will give you his instructions. That's all I
have to say this evening. But I'd like to remind you of
General Yamashita's motto:" Be happy in your work." Just
bear that in mind.'

Saito left the platform and walked back to his headquarters with long angry strides. The prisoners dismissed and
returned to their lines, with the incoherent speech still
ringing unpleasantly in their ears.

'He doesn't seem to have understood, sir. It looks as if
we'll have to fall back on the Hague Convention after all,'
said Clipton to Colonel Nicholson, who had remained silently
wrapped in thought.

'I believe you're right, Clipton,' the Colonel solemnly replied, 'and I'm afraid we're in for a rather stormy passage.'

IV

At one moment Clipton thought that the stormy passage
which Colonel Nicholson had forecast was going to be a
short one and would end, almost before it had begun, in
terrible tragedy. As an M.O., he was the only officer who
was not directly involved in the fuss. Already up to his eyes
in work looking after the countless casualties due to exposure in the jungle, he was not included in the labour
corps; but this only served to intensify his fear when he
witnessed the first clash from the building pompously
labelled 'Hospital,' where he had reported for duty before
dawn.

Woken up while it was still dark by the whistles and the
shouts of the guards, the men had gone on parade in an
ugly mood, still fuddled and not yet fully recovered from
the effects of the mosquitoes and the wretched quarters.
The officers had fallen in where they were told. Colonel

Nicholson had given them definite instructions.

'We must co-operate,' he had said, 'as far as is compatible with our sense of honour. I, too, shall go on parade.'

It was understood that obedience to Saito's orders would go no further than that.

They were kept there for some time, standing to attention in the cold and damp; then, as the sun rose, they saw Colonel Saito appear, surrounded by junior officers and walking in front of the engineer who was to direct the working parties. He seemed to be in a bad mood, but beamed as soon as he saw the British officers lined up behind their commanding officer.

A truck full of tools brought up the rear. While the engineer was supervising the issue of these, Colonel Nicholson stepped one pace forward and asked to speak to Saito. The latter's face clouded over. He said nothing, but the Colonel pretended to regard this silence as a sign of assent and went forward to meet him.

Clipton could not follow his movements, for he had his back to him. But after a bit he came into view, sideways on, and the M.O. saw him wave a little book in the Jap's face, drawing his attention to one particular paragraph—in the *Manual of Military Law*, no doubt. Saito was taken aback. For a moment Clipton thought that a good night's sleep might have put him in a better frame of mind, but he soon saw what a vain hope that was. After the speech he had made the previous evening, even if he was no longer in a bad temper, the vital importance of 'saving face' now dictated his conduct. He went purple with anger. He had expected to have heard the last of this business, and here was the Colonel bringing it up all over again. Such obstinacy drove him all of a sudden into a fit of raving hysteria. Colonel Nicholson was calmly reading, running his finger along each line, unaware of the transformation that had taken place. Clipton, who could see the change in the Jap's expression, almost shouted out loud to warn his C.O. It was too late. With two swift strokes Saito had sent the book flying and slapped the Colonel in the face. He was now standing straight in front of him, bending forward, his eyes popping out of his head, flinging his arms about and yelling abuse in a grotesque mixture of English and Japanese.

In spite of his surprise—for he had not expected this re-action—Colonel Nicholson kept his head. He picked up his book, which had fallen into the mud, stood up again in front of the Jap, over whom he towered head and shoulders, then calmly announced:

'In that case, Colonel Saito, since the Japanese authorities refuse to abide by the laws in force in the rest of the civilised world, we consider ourselves absolved from our duty to obey you. It only remains for me to let you know what orders I've given. My officers will not do manual labour.'

Having said this, he suffered without a murmur a second, still more savage, attack. Saito, who seemed to have gone beserk, leapt at him and, standing on tip-toe, hammered away at the Colonel's face with his fists.

The situation was beginning to get out of hand. Some of the British officers stepped out of the ranks and advanced in a threatening manner. An angry growl rose from the rest of the unit. The Japanese N.C.O.s shouted a word of command, and the soldiers cocked their rifles. Colonel Nicholson asked his officers to fall in again and ordered his men to stay where they were. Blood was pouring from his mouth, but he still preserved his air of authority, which nothing could alter.

Saito, panting hard, stepped back and made as if to seize his revolver; then he seemed to think better of it. He stepped further back and issued an order in an ominously controlled tone of voice. The Japanese guards surrounded the prisoners and motioned them forward. They marched them off in the direction of the river, to the building-yards. There were one or two protests and a slight show of resistance. A few anxi-ous glances of enquiry were fixed on the Colonel, who made it clear he wanted them to obey the order. They eventually disappeared, and the British officers were left alone on the parade ground, facing Colonel Saito.

The Jap started talking again, in measured tones which

Clipton found unnerving. His fears were not groundless. Some soldiers went off and came back with the two machine-guns which were kept at the main gate of the camp. They set them up, one on either side of Saito. Clipton's uneasiness turned to cold terror. He had a view of the whole scene through the bamboo partition of his 'hospital.' Behind him, lying in heaps, were a score of wretches covered in open sores. Some had dragged themselves forward and were looking on as well. One of them gave a hoarse cry:

'Doc, they're not going to . . . surely they can't? That yellow baboon wouldn't dare! But the old man's sticking to his guns!'

Clipton thought it was quite likely that the yellow baboon would dare. Most of the officers standing behind the Colonel were of the same opinion. Mass executions had taken place at the fall of Singapore. Saito had obviously ordered the men off the parade ground so that there should be no tiresome witnesses. He was now speaking in English, ordering the officers to pick up the tools and report for duty.

Colonel Nicholson's voice made itself heard again. He repeated his refusal. No one moved. Saito gave another order. Ammunition belts were slipped in and the guns were trained on the squad.

'Doc,' sobbed the soldier standing next to Clipton, 'Doc, the old man won't give in. I'm telling you, he don't understand. We've got to do something.'

These words spurred Clipton into action; until then he had felt half-paralysed. It was quite clear that the 'old man' did not appreciate the situation. He did not for a moment doubt that Saito would stop at nothing. Something had to be done, as the soldier said; the 'old man' had to be told that he could not sacrifice the lives of twenty others out of sheer stubbornness and for the sake of his principles; that neither his honour nor personal dignity would suffer as a result of giving in to brute force, as everyone else in the other camps had done. The words were on the tip of his tongue. He rushed outside, shouting to Saito.

'Wait a moment, Colonel, wait; I'll tell him!'

Colonel Nicholson rebuked him with a frown.

'That'll do, Clipton. There's nothing more to be said. I'm quite aware of what I'm doing.'

In any case Clipton had not succeeded in getting as far as the squad. Two guards had seized him and pinned him down. But his violent outburst seemed to have made Saito think twice before taking action. Clipton yelled at him, in a rapid torrent of words, so that the other Japanese should not understand.

'I warn you, Colonel, I witnessed the whole scene; and so did the forty men in hospital. You won't succeed in inciting us into a general riot or a mass attempt to escape.'

This was the last desperate card in his hand. Even in the eyes of the Japanese authorities Saito would not be able to justify such an unwarranted execution. He could not afford to leave any British witness alive. Following this argument to its logical conclusion, he would either have to massacre everyone on the sick-list, including the M.O., or else abandon all thought of revenge.

Clipton felt he had scored a temporary victory. Saito appeared to give the matter a great deal of thought. He was choking with rage and the shame of defeat, but he did not order his men to fire.

In fact he gave no order at all. The men remained where they were, with their machine-guns trained on the squad. They remained like that for a long time, a very long time indeed; for Saito refused to 'lose face' by ordering them to dismiss. They remained there for the most of the morning, without daring to move, until the parade ground was completely deserted.

It was hardly a decisive victory, and Clipton could not bear to think of what lay in store for the recalcitrants. But there was some consolation in the thought that he saved them from their immediate fate. The officers were marched off to the prison camp under escort. Colonel Nicholson was dragged away by a couple of gigantic Koreans, who were part of Saito's personal bodyguard. He was taken into the Japanese colonel's office, a small room which opened out on to his sleeping quarters, thus enabling him to pay frequent visits to his store of drink next door. Saito slowly followed his prisoner inside and carefully closed the door behind him. Shortly afterwards Clipton who was a sensitive man at heart, shuddered as he heard the sound of blows.

V

After half an hour's beating-up the Colonel was thrown into a hut where there was neither bed nor chair, so that he was forced to lie down in the damp mud on the floor when he felt too tired to stand up. For food he was given a bowl of rice heavily laced with salt, and Saito warned him that he would keep him there until he decided to obey orders.

For a week the only person he saw was a Korean sentry, a brute who looked like a gorilla, who on his own initiative added still more salt to the daily rice-ration. But he forced himself to swallow a few mouthfuls of it and, after gulping down the whole of his meagre ration of water, he would then lie down on the floor and try to disregard his hardships. He was forbidden to leave the cell, which consequently became as offensive as a cess-pit.

At the end of a week Clipton was at last given permission to visit him. Shortly before, the M.O. had been summoned by Saito, whom he found wearing the sullen expression of an anxious tyrant. He could see that he was wavering between anger and fear, which he did his best to mask behind a cool tone of voice.

'I'm not responsible for all this,' he said. 'The bridge across the river has got to be built, and a Japanese officer can't afford to put up with heroics. Try and make him understand that I don't intend to give in. Tell him that, thanks to him, all his officers are having the same treatment. If that's not enough, his men will have to bear the consequences of his pig-headedness as well. So far I haven't interfered with you, or with those on the sick-list. I've been kind enough to let them off all duties. I shall regard this kindness as a sign of weakness, unless he changes his mind.'

He dismissed him with this threat, and Clipton was taken in to see the prisoner. He was at first horrified by the condition to which the C.O. had been reduced and by the physical deterioration which his body had undergone in such a short time. The sound of his voice, which was barely audible, seemed to be a distant, muffled echo of the tone of authority which the M.O. remembered. But this metamorphosis was only superficial. Colonel Nicholson's spirit had not changed at all; and the words he uttered were still the same, although delivered in a different tone. Clipton, who had fully intended to persuade him to give in, now saw there was no chance of that. He soon exhausted all his carefully prepared arguments, then fell silent. The Colonel did not even answer him, but simply said:

'Please let the others know that I'm still quite adamant. On no account will I have an officer from my battalion working like a navvy.'

Clipton left the cell, torn once again between admiration and anger, a prey to painful indecision, unable to make up his mind whether he should worship the C.O. as a hero or regard him as a complete fool. He wondered whether it would not be best to ask God to crown this dangerous lunatic with a martyr's halo and admit him into His kingdom as quickly as possible, so as to prevent him from turn-the River Kwai camp into a scene of frightful tragedy. What Saito had said was no more than the truth. The treatment being meted out to the other officers was only one degree less inhuman, while the men were made regular targets for the brutality of the guards. As he walked away, Clipton thought of the danger that threatened his patients.

Saito must have been waiting for him, for he rushed up, his eyes betraying genuine anxiety as he enquired:

'Well?'

He was quite sober, and looked rather depressed. Clipton tried to judge how far the Colonel's attitude was likely to make the Jap 'lose face,' then pulled himself together and decided to take a firm line.

'Well, it's like this. Colonel Nicholson won't give in to force, nor will his officers. And in view of the way he's being treated, I could not advise him to do so.'

He protested against the conditions of the prisoners in detention, quoting the Hague Convention as the Colonel had done, arguing from his professional point of view as a doctor and finally from the simple humanitarian point of view, even going so far as to declare that such monstrous treatment was tantamount to murder. He expected a violent reaction, but none came. Saito merely muttered that the Colonel was to blame for the whole business, and then abruptly walked off. At that moment Clipton felt inclined to believe that he was really not such a bad man at heart, and that his actions were all due to fear of one kind or another: fear of his superiors, who were probably badgering him about the bridge, and fear of his subordinates, in whose eyes he was 'losing face' through his obvious inability to exact obedience.

His natural inclination to generalise led Clipton to identify this combination of two fears, the fear of superiors and of subordinates respectively, as the main source of all human calamities. As he put this idea into words, he felt that somewhere or other he had once come across this very psychological maxim. This gave him a certain sense of satisfaction, which helped to allay his anxiety. He developed this train of thought a little further, but was brought to a stop on the threshold of the hospital by the realisation that every calamity, even the worst in the world, could be attributed to men who had neither superiors nor subordinates.

Saito must have thought the matter over. His treatment of the prisoner was more lenient during the following week, at the end of which he went to see him and asked if he had finally decided to behave like a gentleman. He had arrived in a reasonable frame of mind, intending to appeal to the Colonel's common sense, but faced with the latter's refusal to discuss a question which was already cut-and-dried he again lost his temper and worked himself up into a state of hysterical frenzy in which he could hardly be taken for a civilised human being. The Colonel was again beaten up, and the gorilla-like Korean received strict orders for the harsh régime of the first few days to be resumed. Saito even struck the guard as well. He was no longer responsible for his actions when seized by these fits, and he accused the man of being too soft-hearted. He rushed about the cell like a raving lunatic, brandishing a pistol and threatening to use it on the guard as well as the prisoner in order to enforce a little discipline.

Clipton, who once more tried to intervene, also came in for a few blows, and his hospital was cleared of all patients who were still capable of standing upright. They were forced to drag themselves to the building-yards and shift heavy loads; otherwise they would have been beaten to death. For several days terror reigned over the River Kwai camp. Colonel Nicholson's answer to his ill-treatment was a stubborn, haughty silence.

Saito's personality seemed to switch from that of a Mister Hyde, capable of every kind of atrocity, to a comparatively humane Doctor Jekyll. Once the period of violence was over, a régime of extraordinary leniency succeeded it. Colonel Nicholson was allowed to draw not only full rations but also a supplementary scale normally earmarked for the sick-list. Clipton was given permission to see him and attend to him, and Saito even warned him that he hold him personally responsible for the Colonel's health.

One evening Saito had the prisoner brought into his room and then ordered the escort to dismiss. Alone with him, he asked him to sit down and drew from his stores a tin of American corned beef, some cigarettes and a bottle of liqueur whisky. He told him that, as a soldier, he felt a deep admiration for his attitude, but war was war even though neither of them was responsible for it. Surely he could understand that he, Saito, was obliged to obey the orders of his superior officers? Now these orders stated that the bridge across the River Kwai was to be built as quickly as possible. He was therefore compelled to make use of all the personnel available. The Colonel refused the corned beef, the cigarettes and the whisky but listened with interest to what he had to say. He calmly replied that Saito had not the foggiest idea of how to tackle a work of such importance.

He had reverted to his original arguments. It looked as though the squabble was likely to go on forever. No one on earth could have told whether Saito was going to discuss the matter sensibly or give vent to another hysterical outburst. He was silent for some time, while the question no doubt was being debated on some supernatural plane unknown to mere mortals. The Colonel took advantage of this and said:

'May I ask you, Colonel Saito, if you're satisfied with the work so far?'

The insidious question might well have tipped the scales on the side of hysteria, for the work was progressing badly —which was one of Colonel Saito's major worries, since his career was at stake as much as his reputation. But this was not the cue for Mister Hyde. He looked foolish, hung his head and muttered some inaudible reply. Then he put a full glass of whisky into the prisoner's hand, poured a large one out for himself and said:

'Look, Colonel Nicholson, I don't think you've really understood. There's no need for us to be at loggerheads. When I said all the officers were to work, naturally I never meant you, the Commanding Officer. My orders only applied to the others . . .'

'Not one of my officers will work,' said the Colonel, putting his glass back on the table.

Saito suppressed a gesture of annoyance and concentrated on keeping calm.

'I've been thinking the matter over during the last few days,' he went on. 'I think I could put majors and above on administrative duties. Only the junior officers would then have to lend a hand . . .'

'None of the officers will do any manual labour,' said Colonel Nicholson. 'An officer must be in command of his men.'

At this Saito could control himself no longer. But when

the Colonel returned to his cell, having successfully stuck to his guns in spite of bribes, threats, blows and even entreaties, he felt that the situation was well in hand and that it would not be long before the enemy capitulated.

VI

The work was at a standstill. The Colonel had touched Saito on a raw spot when he asked how the task was progressing, and he was proved right in his forecast that the Japanese would eventually have to yield through sheer necessity.

Three weeks had gone by, and not only was the bridge not yet under way, but the preliminary preparations had been handled so ingeniously by the prisoners that it would take considerable time to repair all the damage that had been done.

Infuriated by the treatment meted out to the C.O., whose courage and endurance they had admired, fretting under the torrent of curses and blows which the sentries rained down on them, indignant at being employed like slaves on work which was useful to the enemy, feeling all at sea now that they were separated from their officers and no longer heard the familiar words of command, the British soldiers competed with each other to see who could be the slackest or, better still, who could commit the most elementary blunders under an ostentatious show of keenness.

There was no punishment sufficiently severe to curb their insidious activities, and the little Japanese engineer was sometimes reduced to tears of desperation. The guards were too thin on the ground to superintend all of them, and too stupid to spot the culprits. The lay-out of the two stretches of line had had to be started all over again at least twenty times. Both the straight sections and the curves, which had been accurately computed and pegged out by the engineer, would relapse as soon as his back was turned into a maze of disconnected lines diverging at sharp angles, at which he would afterwards cry out in despair. The two bits on either side of the river, which the bridge was eventually meant to connect, were palpably at a different level and never ended up directly opposite each other. One of the squads would then start digging furiously and succeed in producing a sort of crater which dipped far lower than the level required, while the fool of a guard would gaze with delight at the sight of such feverish activity. When the engineer turned up he would lose his temper, and beat guards and prisoners indiscriminately. The former, realising they had been fooled once again, would take their revenge; but the harm had been done, and it took several hours or several days to repair it.

One squad had been ordered to cut down some trees as timber for the bridge. They would make a careful selection and bring back the most twisted and brittle ones they could find; or else devote considerable effort to felling a giant tree, which would subsequently tumble into the river and be lost. Or again, they would choose trunks which were eaten away inside by insects and collapsed under the slightest weight.

Saito, who carried out a daily inspection, gave vent to his fury in increasingly stormy outbursts of temper. He dispensed curses, threats and blows, swearing even at the engineer, who would answer back with the retort that the fatigue parties were absolutely useless. At which he would scream and swear louder than ever and try to think of a new form of punishment to put an end to this sullen resistance. He made the prisoners suffer more than if he had been an embittered jailer left to his own devices and scared stiff of being sacked for inefficiency. Those who were caught red-handed in an act of wilful damage or sabotage were tied to trees, beaten with thorn-branches and left out in the open for hours, bleeding and naked, exposed to the ants and the tropical sun. Clipton saw the victims as they came back in the evening; they were carried in by their pals, shaking with fever, their backs stripped raw. He was not even allowed to keep them on the sick list for long. Saito did not forget who they were. As soon as they were capable of standing, he sent them back to work and ordered the guards to keep a special eye on them.

The moral fibre shown by these 'bad-hats' was so moving that Clipton sometimes found himself in tears. He was amazed to see them take such punishment. There was always at least one of them who, when he was alone with him, would find the strength to sit up with a cheerful wink and whisper a few words.

The most brutal forms of punishment had achieved no result whatever. The men had got used to them. The example set by Colonel Nicholson was a stimulant even stronger than the beer and whisky which they no longer had to drink. If one of them was ever punished beyond the limits of human endurance and could only go on working at the risk of his life, there was always another ready to relieve him. This was a recognised routine.

In Clipton's opinion, they were even more to be praised for refusing to be taken in by the mealy-mouthed promises which Saito made during those fits of depression when he realised he had exhausted every known form of torture and was incapable of inventing others.

One day he made them parade outside his office, having ordered them to stop work earlier than usual—so as not to overtire them, he explained. He issued them all with rice-cakes and fruit bought from the Siamese peasants in the nearest village—a gift from the Japanese army to spur them on to greater efforts. He abandoned all sense of shame and positively grovelled in front of them. He prided himself, he told them, on being one of them, just an ordinary sort of chap, whose only wish was to do his duty with as little fuss as possible. Their officers, he pointed out, were making them all work twice as hard by refusing to work themselves. So he fully understood how resentful they must feel, and did not hold it against them. On the contrary, in order to show his sympathy for them, he had on his own authority reduced the individual quota of work on the embankment. The engineer had fixed this as one and a half cubic yards of earth per man; well, he, Saito, had decided to make it one cubic yard. He was doing this because he felt sorry for them in their present condition, for which he himself was not to blame. He hoped that, in view of this kindly gesture, they would co-operate with him and speed up this easy work, which would help to bring the damn war to an end.

He was almost pleading with them by the time he had finished, but his prayers and entreaties had no more effect than his curses and blows. Next day the quota was fulfilled. Each man conscientiously dug up and carted off his cubic yard of earth; some even more. But the distance they carried it was an insult to the meanest intelligence.

Saito was the first to yield. He was at the end of his tether; the prisoners' sustained resistance had reduced him to a pitiful condition. He spent the days preceding his final downfall prowling about the camp with the same desperate look in his eye as a beast at bay. He even went so far as to ask the young subalterns to choose for themselves what work they wanted to do, promising them special privileges and extra rations. But they all stood firm and, since a high-level Japanese inspection was imminent, he resigned himself to ignominious surrender.

He prepared to make one last desperate bid to 'save face' and cover up his defeat, but this pathetic attempt did not even deceive his own men. The 7th of December, 1942, being the anniversary of Japan's entry into the war, he announced that in honour of the occasion he had undertaken to grant a general amnesty. He had an interview with the Colonel and told him he had adopted a measure of extreme benevolence: all officers would henceforth be exempt from manual labour. In return for this he trusted they would devote themselves to supervising their men's activity so as to ensure the maximum efficiency.

Colonel Nicholson replied that he would see what could be done. Now that the situation was established on a proper constitutional basis there was no longer any reason for trying to oppose the enemy programme. As in every civilised army, the officers—it went without saying—would be responsible for the conduct of their men.

This was total surrender on the part of the Japanese. That evening the victory was celebrated in the British camp by a sing-song, cheers and an extra rice-ration, which had been issued with the greatest reluctance on Saito's orders, as a further gesture of goodwill. That same evening the Japanese colonel retired earlier than usual, wept for his loss of face and drowned his sorrows in a bout of solitary drinking which lasted well into the night; until he slumped dead-drunk on to his bed—a state which he hardly ever managed to reach except in unusual circumstances; for he had an amazingly strong head and could normally stand the most barbaric mixtures.

VII

Colonel Nicholson, accompanied by his usual advisers, Major Hughes and Captain Reeves, went down to the river along the railway embankment on which the prisoners were at work.

He walked slowly. He was in no hurry. Immediately after his release he had scored a second victory by obtaining four days off duty for his officers and himself by way of compensation for their unjust punishment. Saito had clenched his fists at the thought of this further delay, but had given in. He had even issued orders for the prisoners to be decently treated, and had bashed in the face of one of his own soldiers whom he had caught smiling sarcastically.

If Colonel Nicholson had applied for four days' exemption from duty, it was not only to recover his strength; it was also to give him time to think, to sum up the situation, to hold discussions with his staff and draw up a plan of action, steps which every conscientious commander should take instead of rushing bald-headed at the easiest solution—a thing he hated doing more than anything else in the world.

It did not take him long to spot the outrageous mistakes

intentionally committed by his men. Hughes and Reeves could not suppress a cry of admiration when they saw the astonishing results of this activity.

'That's a fine embankment for a railway line!' said Hughes. 'I suggest you put the culprits up for a decoration, sir. Just think of an ammunition train trundling over that lot!'

The Colonel did not even smile.

'A splendid job, sir,' echoed Captain Reeves, the ex-Public Works engineer. 'No one in his senses could possibly imagine they intend to run a railway over this switchback. I'd sooner face the Japanese army all over again than take a trip along this line.'

The Colonel looked as solemn as ever and asked:

'In your opinion, Reeves, your opinion as a technician, could this be put to any use at all?'

'I don't think so, sir,' Reeves answered after a moment's reflection. 'They'd do better to abandon this mess completely and build another line a little further up.'

Colonel Nicholson looked more and more preoccupied. He nodded his head and moved on in silence. He wanted to see the whole of the building-yards before forming an opinion.

He reached the river. A squad of about fifty men, stark naked except for the triangle of cloth which the Japanese called 'working-kit,' were milling about on the stretch under construction. A guard, with a rifle slung, marched up and down in front of them. Some of the squad were engaged on digging a little further away, while the remainder were busy collecting the earth on bamboo carriers and spreading it out on either side of a line marked out with white pegs. This had originally run at right-angles to the bank, but the insidious genius of the prisoners had succeeded in shifting it so that it was now almost parallel to the river. The Japanese engineer was not on the spot. He could be seen on the opposite bank gesticulating in the middle of another squad, who were taken across the river every morning on rafts. He could also be heard.

'Who set out that line of pegs?' the Colonel asked,

coming to a standstill.

'He did, sir,' said the British corporal, springing to attention and pointing to the engineer. 'He set it out, but I helped him a little myself. I made a slight improvement as soon as he left. He and I don't always see eye to eye, sir.'

And, since the sentry was not looking, he gave a conspiratorial wink. Colonel Nicholson did not acknowledge this secret message, but remained deep in thought.

'I see,' he said in a voice as cold as ice.

He moved on without further comment and stopped in front of another corporal. This one, with the help of a few men, was devoting considerable effort to clearing the ground of a number of large roots by heaving them up to the top of a slope instead of pitching them down the side of the bank, while another Japanese guard blankly looked on.

'How many are at work in this squad to-day?' the Colonel asked in ringing tones.

The guard gaped at him, wondering if it was in order for the Colonel to speak like this to the prisoners; but his voice held such a note of authority that he did not dare move. The corporal at once sprang to attention and began to stammer a reply.

'Twenty or twenty-five, sir, I'm not quite sure. One man went sick as soon as we arrived. He suddenly felt dizzy— I can't think why, sir, for he was perfectly all right at reveille. Three or four of the lads were needed, of course, to carry him to hospital, sir, as he couldn't walk by himself. They haven't come back yet. He was the biggest and the toughest chap in the squad. As it is, we shan't be able to get through our quota to-day. There seems to be a curse on this railway.'

'A corporal,' said the Colonel, 'ought to know exactly how many men he has under him. What is the quota, anyway?'

'A cubic yard of earth per man per day, sir, to be dug and then carted away. But with these damn roots and all, sir, it looks as if it's going to be too much for us.'

'I see,' said the Colonel as coldly as ever.

He moved off, muttering under his breath through clenched teeth. Hughes and Reeves followed behind him.

They went to the top of a rise, from which they could see the river and the whole of the surrounding country. At that point the Kwai was over a hundred yards wide, with both banks high above the level of the water. The Colonel studied the ground from every angle, then turned to his two subordinates. What he had to say was obvious, but he said it in a voice which had recovered all its former tone of authority.

'These people, the Japanese, have only just emerged from a state of barbarism, and prematurely at that. They've tried to copy our methods, but they don't understand them. Take away their model, and they're lost. They can't even do the job they've taken on here in this valley, yet it doesn't need much intelligence. They don't realise they'd save time by planning in advance instead of rushing bald-headed at the thing. What do you think, Reeves? Railways and bridges are in your line, aren't they?'

'You're quite right, sir,' said the Captain, instinctively warming to his subject. 'I've tackled at least a dozen jobs like this in India. With the material available in the jungle and the personnel that we've got here, a qualified engineer could build this bridge in under six months. There are times, I'm afraid, when their incompetence simply makes my blood boil.'

'I agree,' said Hughes. 'I can't help it, but I sometimes feel like screaming at the sight of such inefficiency. You'd think it was quite simple to——'

'What about me?' the Colonel broke in. 'Do you think I'm pleased with this scandalous state of affairs? I'm absolutely appalled by what I've seen this morning.'

'Well, anyway, sir,' laughed Captain Reeves, 'I don't think we need worry about the invasion of India if this is the line they say they're going to use. The bridge across the Kwai is not quite ready to take the weight of their trains!'

Colonel Nicholson was deep in thought, but he kept his blue eyes firmly fixed on his two companions.

'Gentlemen,' he said, 'I can see we'll have to take a very

firm line if we want to regain control of the men. Through
these savages they've fallen into idle, slipshod habits unbe-
coming to members of His Majesty's forces. We'll have to
be patient with them and handle them carefully, for they
can't be held directly responsible for the present state of
affairs. What they need is discipline, and they haven't had
it. It's no good using violence instead. You've only got to
look at the result—a lot of disconnected activity, but not
a single positive achievement. These Orientals have shown
how incompetent they are, when it comes to man-management.[1]

There was a moment's silence while the two officers
wondered what he really meant by these remarks. But they
were quite clear; there was nothing to read between the
lines. The Colonel had spoken in his usual forthright
manner. He let his words sink in and then went on:

'I must ask you, therefore—and I'll ask all the other
officers as well—to show as much consideration as possible
at first. But on no account must our patience be stretched
to the point of weakness, or else we'll fall to the level of
these brutes. I shall also speak to the men myself. As from
to-day we've got to put a stop to this disgraceful inefficiency. We can't have the men going absent on the
slightest provocation. The N.C.O.s must answer any question put to them promptly and clearly. I don't think I need
remind you of the need for firm action at the first sign
of sabotage or malingering. A railway line is meant to run
horizontally and not twist about like a switchback, as you
so rightly observed, Reeves . . [2]

PART TWO

I

In Calcutta Colonel Green, commanding Force 316, was studying a report which had just come in by the usual roundabout route, a report embellished with the marginal comments of half a dozen military and para-military clandestine services. Force 316 (better known as 'The Plastic and Destructions Co., Ltd.') had not yet reached the important position that it later held in the Far East, but it was already taking an active, passionate and exclusive interest in Japanese war establishment in the occupied countries of Malaya, Burma, Siam and China. What it lacked in material resources, it tried to make up for by the boldness and dash of its agents.

'Well, it's the first time I've ever known them all to agree.' Colonel Green muttered. 'We ought to do something about it.'

The first part of his remark referred to the various clandestine services associated with Force 316, each working in a separate watertight compartment and pursuing an individual policy of its own, with the result that they often came to widely different conclusions. This used to infuriate Colonel Green, who was responsible for planning operations from all the intelligence available. 'Ops' was the preserve of Force 316; Colonel Green was not interested in theoretical discussion except in so far as it affected his own line of action. His staff were quite familiar with his views on the matter since he expressed them at least once a day. A large part of his time was spent in trying to sift the truth from these reports, taking into account not only the information itself but also the psychological make-up of the various sources (optimism or pessimism, tendency to exaggerate the facts, or on the other hand, complete inability to interpret them).

Colonel Green had a special grievance against the genuine, the great, the famous, the one and only Intelligence Service, which regarded itself as an exclusively intellectual body and systematically refused to co-operate with the operational staff. Instead, it locked itself up in its own ivory tower, never let its precious documents be seen by anyone who could have made use of them, on the pretext that they were too secret, and carefully filed them away in a safe. There they remained for years, until they were no longer of use to anyone—or, to be more precise, until long after the end of the war, when one of the big-wigs felt an urge to write his memoirs before dying, to leave something to posterity and disclose to an astonished nation how clever the Service had been on one particular date and on one particular occasion, when it ascertained every detail of the enemy plan of campaign : the place and time of the impending attack had been accurately determined in advance. The forecast was a hundred per cent correct, since the enemy had indeed struck in the manner foretold, and with the success that had likewise been foreseen.

That at least was how it appeared, in a rather exaggerated light perhaps, to Colonel Green, who disagreed with the theory of art for art's sake being applied to intelligence matters. He muttered some inaudible remark as he thought of some of the previous ventures; then, in view of the miraculous unanimous agreement on the present scheme, it was almost with disappointment that he felt he had to admit that for once the services had done something useful. He consoled himself with the thought—not entirely a fair one—that the information contained in the report had been known to everyone in India for years. Finally he went through it again and made a mental summary of it, with the idea of taking action on it.

'The Burma-Siam railway is now under construction. Sixty thousand Allied prisoners, drafted by the Japanese into labour corps, are being employed on it and are working under ghastly conditions. In spite of appalling losses, it is calculated that the task, which is of considerable importance to the enemy, will be completed in a few months. Herewith a rough sketch-map. It shows several river-crossings by means of wooden bridges . . .'

At this point in his summary Colonel Green felt in good form again and almost grinned with pleasure. He went on:

'The Siamese people are extremely discontented with the "liberators," who have requisitioned all the rice and whose troops behave as though they were in occupied territory. The peasants in the railway area in particular are showing signs of unrest. Several senior officers in the Siamese army, and even some members of the royal family, have recently established contact with the Allies and are prepared to launch an anti-Japanese underground movement, for which countless peasants have volunteered. They request both weapons and instructors.'

'No doubt about it,' Colonel Green decided, 'I'll have to send a team into the railway area.'

Having made his decision, he pondered for some time on the various qualities that would be required by the leader of such an expedition. After ruling out a number of possible candidates, he called for Major Shears, an ex-cavalry officer who had been transferred to Force 316 at the time that special unit had been formed and was, in fact, one of its founder-members. This private army had only seen the light of day thanks to the persistent efforts of a few individualists and the reluctant support of a handful of military experts. Shears had only just arrived from Europe, where he had successfully completed several tricky missions, when he had his lengthy interview with Colonel Green. The Colonel gave him all the information available and outlined the general purpose of his mission.

'You'll take only a few stores in with you,' he said, 'the rest will be dropped to you as and when you need them. About the actual operation, you'll be able to see for yourself on the spot, but don't be in too much of a hurry. I think it'll be best to wait till the railway's finished and deliver a single powerful blow rather than risk giving the whole show away by a series of minor attacks.'

There was no need to specify what form the 'operation' would take or what type of stores would be used. The *raison d'être* of 'The Plastic and Destructions Co., Ltd.' made a fuller explanation superfluous.

Meanwhile, Shears was to get in touch with the Siamese, make sure of their good intentions and loyalty, then start training the partisans.

'As I see it, you'll need to be a team of three,' said Colonel Green, 'for the moment at any rate. How does that strike you?'

'That seems quite reasonable, sir,' Shears agreed. 'We need at least a nucleus of three Europeans. Any more, and we might present too big a target.'

'That's settled, then. Who do you plan to take in with you?'

'I suggest Warden, sir.'

'Captain Warden? Professor Warden? You certainly don't believe in half-measures, Shears. With you, that'll make two of our best agents.'

'I understood it was an important mission, sir,' was Shears's non-committal reply.

'It is. It's a very important mission, from the political as well as the operational point of view.'

'Warden's just the man for that, sir. An ex-professor of Oriental languages. He speaks Siamese and will be able to get on with the natives. He's a level-headed sort of chap and doesn't get the wind up—at least not more than most of us.'

'You can have Warden. Now what about the third?'

'I'll think it over, sir. Probably one of the youngsters who've been through the course. I've seen several who look quite promising. I'll let you know to-morrow.'

Force 316 had established a school in Calcutta where the young volunteers were trained.

'Right. Here's the map. I've marked the possible D.Z.s and hide-outs where the Siamese say you'll be able to lie up without any risk of being discovered. We've already done the air reconnaissance.'

Shears bent over the map and the aerial photographs. He carefully studied the area which Force 316 had chosen as his theatre of unorthodox activity in the wilds of Siam. He felt the thrill which seized him each time he embarked on a new expedition into unknown territory. There was something exciting about any Force 316 mission, but this time the attraction was intensified by the wild nature of the jungle-clad mountains inhabited by lawless tribes of hunters.

'There seem to be several suitable spots,' Colonel Green went on. 'For instance, this isolated little hamlet not far from the Burmese border, about two or three days' march from the railway, apparently. According to the sketch-map, the railway there crosses a river—the River Kwai, if the map's right. The bridge there will probably be one of the longest on the line.'

Shears smiled, as his C.O. had done, at the thought of the number of bridges across the river.

'I'll have to study the question more closely, of course; but for the moment, sir, I should think that place would make a perfect H.Q.'

'Right. Now all we've got to do is arrange for the drop. That'll be in three or four weeks, I should think, if the Siamese agree. Ever done a jump?'

'Never, sir. Parachuting wasn't included in the course until after I'd left Europe. I don't think Warden has, either.'

'Hang on a moment. I'll see if the experts can put you through a few training jumps.'

Colonel Green seized the telephone, asked for a certain R.A.F. office and told them what he wanted. He listened for some time and did not seem at all pleased with what he heard. Shears, who kept his eyes on him throughout the conversation, could see how his mood changed.

'That's really your considered opinion, then?' Colonel Green asked.

He frowned as he listened to the reply, then hung up the receiver. After a moment's hesitation, he finally made up his mind and said:

'Do you want to know the experts' opinion? It's this. They just said: "If you absolutely insist on your chaps doing some training jumps, we'll make the necessary arrangements. But we honestly wouldn't advise it—not unless they can spare six months for a proper course. Our experience of missions dropping into this sort of country can be summed up as follows: if they do only one jump, you know, there's a fifty per cent chance of an injury. Two jumps, it's eighty per cent. The third time, it's dead certain they won't get off scot free. You see? It's not a question of training, but the law of averages. The wisest thing would be for them to do just the one jump—and hope for the best." Well, that's what they said. Now it's up to you.'

'One of the great advantages of the modern army, sir,' Shears calmly replied, 'is that there are experts to solve all the problems for us. It's no good thinking that we know better than them. What they've said obviously shows common sense as well. I'm sure it will appeal to Warden's logical mind; he's bound to agree with it. We'll take the advice and do the one jump—and hope for the best.'

II

'You don't look altogether happy, Reeves,' said Colonel Nicholson to the R.E. captain, whose face showed every sign of suppressed anger. 'What's wrong?'

'What's wrong! We simply can't go on like this, sir! I tell you, it's hopeless! I'd already decided to approach you on the subject to-day. And here's Major Hughes who'll back me up.'

'What's wrong?' the Colonel repeated with a frown.

'I agree with Reeves completely, sir,' said Hughes, who had left the building-yards to join the C.O. 'I also wanted to tell you this simply can't go on.'

'But what?'

'It's utter chaos, sir. Never in the whole of my career have I seen such carelessness and lack of system. We're getting nowhere like this, just marking time. Everyone gives contradictory orders. These fellows, the Japs, haven't the vaguest idea of man-management. If they insist on inter-fering with the work, there's not a hope of ever getting it done.'

The situation had certainly improved since the British officers had been put in charge of the squads, but although there were noticeable signs of progress in the quality as well as the quantity of the work, it was quite clear that things were far from perfect.

'Explain yourselves. You first, Reeves.'

'Sir,' said the captain, taking a sheet of paper out of his pocket, 'I've only made a note of the more glaring blunders; otherwise the list would go on forever.'

'Go ahead. I'm here to listen to any reasonable complaint, and to consider any suggestion. I can see there's something wrong. It's up to you to tell me what.'

'Well, in the first place, sir, it's utter folly to build the bridge on this bit of ground.'

'Why?'

'It's a quagmire, sir. Who ever heard of a railway bridge being built on shifting soil? Only savages like these would ever think of it. I'm willing to bet, sir, that the bridge will collapse the first time a train goes over it.'

'That's rather serious, Reeves,' said the Colonel, keeping his light blue eyes fixed on the junior officer.

'Very serious, sir. And I've tried to point that out to the Japanese engineer. Engineer indeed; God, what a hopeless bungler! You can't get any sense from a chap who's never even heard of a soil resistance, who gapes when you mention pressure tables and who can't even talk the King's English. Yet I've been pretty patient, sir. I've tried every-thing to make him understand. I even arranged a little demonstration for him, in the hope that he couldn't fail to believe what he saw with his own eyes. Just a waste of time. He still insists on building his bridge in this swamp.'

'A demonstration, Reeves?' asked Colonel Nicholson, whose interest was always aroused at the sound of this word.

'Quite a simple one, sir. A child could have understood it. You see that pile in the water, near the bank? I put that in myself with a sledgehammer. Well, it's gone quite far down already, but it hasn't yet found solid bottom. It's still sinking, sir, just as all the other piles will sink under the weight of a train, I'm sure of it. What we ought to do is lay down a concrete foundation, but we haven't got the materials.'

The Colonel gazed with interest at the pile and asked Reeves if he could repeat the demonstration for his benefit. Reeves gave the necessary orders. Some of the prisoners gathered round and began to heave on a rope. A heavy weight, slung from a scaffolding, dropped once or twice on to the top of the pile, which at once sank visibly deeper.

'You see, sir.' Reeves shouted triumphantly. 'We could go on hammering away till doomsday, it would just go on sinking. And soon it'll be under water.'

'I see,' said the Colonel. 'How far down is it at the moment?'

Reeves gave him the exact figure, which he had noted and added that the tallest trees in the jungle wouldn't be long enough to reach the solid bottom.

'Right,' said the Colonel with every sign of satisfaction. 'That's quite clear. As you say, even a child could understand. That's the sort of demonstration I like. The engineer wasn't impressed? Well, I am—and that's the main thing, I assure you. Now what solution do you suggest?'

'Shift the whole bridge, sir. I think there's a good spot about a mile away. Of course, I'd have to check on it——'

'You must do so then,' the Colonel calmly replied, 'and give me the facts and figures for me to put before them.'

He made a note of this first point and asked:

'Anything else, Reeves?'

'The material they're using on the bridge, sir. Cutting down these trees! That was a fine thing our men started, wasn't it? But at least they knew what they were doing. Well, this hopeless engineer isn't doing much better, sir. He just lets any old thing be cut down, without bothering if the wood's hard or soft, rigid or flexible, or whether it will stand up to any stress laid on it. It's an absolute disgrace, sir.'

Colonel Nicholson made a second entry on the bit of paper which served as a note-book.

'What else, Reeves?'

'I've kept this for the last, sir, because I think it's the most important. You can see for yourself: the river's well over a hundred yards across. It's got high banks. The platform will be over a hundred feet above the water—that's quite a proposition, isn't it? Not child's play. Well, I've asked the engineer several times to show me his working-plans. He shook his head in the usual way, as they all do when they don't know what to say. Well, believe it or not, sir, there isn't a plan! He hasn't made one. And he doesn't intend to! Didn't seem to know what it was all about? So what it boils down to is this: he thinks building a bridge is as easy as throwing a plank across a ditch—some bits of wood here and there, and a few piles underneath! It'll never stand up, sir. I'm absolutely ashamed to be taking part in such sabotage.'

His indignation was so genuine that Colonel Nicholson felt obliged to offer a few words of consolation.

'Don't worry, Reeves. It's a good thing you've got it off your chest. I can quite understand how you feel about it. Everyone has his pride, after all.'

'Exactly, sir. Frankly, I'd rather have another dose of punishment than help to give birth to this monstrosity.'

'I agree with you entirely,' said the Colonel, making a note of this last point. 'It's obviously rather serious, all this, and we can't let things go on as they are. I'll take the necessary steps, I promise you. Your turn now, Hughes.'

Major Hughes was as worked up as his colleague. This was a strange state for him to be in, for by nature he was cool and collected.

'Sir, we'll never get any discipline in the building-yards, or any serious work out of the men, so long as the Japanese guards interfere with our orders—just look at them, sir, absolute oafs. Only this morning I'd split up the squads working on the embankment into three sections each: one for digging, another for carting off the earth, and the third for spreading it and levelling the mound. I'd taken the trouble to arrange the relative strength of each section myself and to organise the various tasks so as to synchronise them properly.'

'I see,' said the Colonel, his interest once more roused. 'A sort of specialisation system?'

'Exactly, sir. After all, I do know something about earthworks. I was a works manager before being a director. I've dug wells over three hundred feet deep. Well, anyway, this morning my teams began working according to this system. Everything was going fine. They were well ahead of the schedule laid down by the Japs. Splendid! Then up comes one of these apes and starts chucking his weight about, shrieking and yelling for the three sections to re-form as one. Easier to keep an eye on them, I suppose—the idiot! What's the result? A complete mess-up, utter chaos. They're all on top of each other and can't get a move on. It's enough to make you sick, sir. Just look at them.'

'You're right, I can see that,' Colonel Nicholson agreed after carefully watching the men at work. 'I'd already noticed the lack of organisation.'

'But that's not all, sir. These idiots have fixed a quota of a cubic yard of earth per man, without realising that our chaps under proper supervision could do much more. Between you and me, sir, it's a soft job. When they think each man has dug, shifted and spread his cubic yard, they call it a day. That's why I say they're idiots. If there are still a few clods of earth left to be carted away so as to connect two isolated stretches, do you think they ask for an extra effort? Not a bit of it! They simply order the squad to down tools. In that case, how can I order them to carry on? What would the men think of me if I did?'

'So you think it's a really poor show?' said Colonel Nicholson.

'It's an absolutely rotten show, sir,' Reeves broke in. 'In India, where the climate's just as bad as this, and the ground's much harder, the coolies get through one and a half cubic yards quite easily.'

'That's what I thought,' the Colonel murmured. 'I was once in charge of a job like this myself, building a road in

Africa. My men used to work much faster than this. One thing's quite clear,' he concluded decisively, 'we can't go on like this. You were quite right to let me know about it.'

He went through his notes again and, after a moment's reflection, turned once more to his two officers:

'Now listen, both of you. Do you know what I think of all this? Practically the whole trouble can be traced back to one simple cause: complete lack of organisation. I'm the first to blame, I know; I should have seen to it in the first place. That's the worst of rushing things, you always waste time in the end. Organisation, plain and simple—that's what we need more than anything else.'

'You've said it, sir,' Hughes agreed. 'A job like this is doomed to failure if it's not properly worked out in advance.'

'I think we'd better call a conference,' said Colonel Nicholson. 'I should have thought of that before. Between the Japanese and us. A discussion between both sides is what we need to determine each man's duties and responsibilities. That's it, a conference. I'll go and have a word with Saito right away.'

III

The conference was held a few days later. Saito did not understand what it was all about, but he had agreed to be present, not daring to ask for an explanation for fear of losing face by appearing ignorant of the customs of a civilisation which he hated but which impressed him in spite of himself.

Colonel Nicholson had drafted an agenda, and waited with his officers in the long hut which served as a dining-room. Saito arrived accompanied by his engineer, some of his bodyguard and three captains, whom he had brought along to swell the numbers in his escort although they could not speak a word of English. The British officers stood up and snapped to attention. The Colonel gave a regimental salute. Saito looked quite startled. He had arrived with the intention of asserting his authority, and here he was, already conscious of his inferiority when faced with this ritual performed with a traditional and majestic sense of propriety.

There was quite a long silence, during which Colonel Nicholson shot a glance of enquiry at the Jap commandant, whom he naturally expected to take the chair. The conference could not be held without a chairman. Out of common courtesy the Colonel felt obliged to wait for the other to declare the meeting open. But Saito felt more and more ill at ease and could hardly bear the idea of being the focal point of this gathering. The manners and customs of the civilised world made him feel small. But he could not allow his subordinates to see that he was unfamiliar with them, and he was paralysed with the fearful thought that he might be committing himself by taking the chair. The little Japanese engineer looked even less self-assured.

With a great effort he pulled himself together. In a churlish tone of voice he asked Colonel Nicholson what he had to say. This was the least compromising move he could think of making. Realising that he would get nothing more out of him, the Colonel decided to take action and embarked on a speech which the English side, with increasing anxiety, had begun to lose hope of ever hearing. He started off with the word 'Gentlemen,' declared the meeting open and in a few words outlined his proposals : to establish a proper organisation for the construction of the River Kwai bridge and to draw up in general terms a plan of action specifying each individual responsibility. Clipton, who was also present—the Colonel had asked him to attend, since the M.O. was naturally concerned with certain points of general administration—noticed that the C.O. had completely recovered his self-assurance and that his confidence asserted itself in direct proportion to Saito's increasing embarrassment.

After a short formal preamble, the Colonel embarked on the main subject and came to the first important point.

'Before tackling any other question, Colonel Saito, we ought to discuss the position of the bridge. It was fixed, I believe, a little hastily and we now think it ought to be changed. We have in mind a point about a mile further downstream. This, of course, would entail an extra stretch of railway line. It would also mean shifting the camp and building new quarters nearer the site. But I don't think we should let this stop us.'

Saito gave a hoarse grunt, and Clipton thought he was going to lose his temper. It was easy to imagine his frame of mind. Time was running short. More than a month had gone by with no material result being achieved, and now came this proposal for a considerable increase in the work as originally envisaged. He stood up suddenly, his hand clutching the hilt of his sword; but Colonel Nicholson gave him no opportunity of continuing this demonstration.

'Just a minute, Colonel Saito,' he said in ringing tones. 'I've had the matter looked into by my colleague, Captain Reeves, an engineer officer who is one of our bridge-building experts. The conclusions he has reached . . .'

Two days before, after carefully watching the Japanese engineer at work, he had been finally convinced of his inefficiency. He had at once taken a definite decision. He had seized his technical adviser by the arm and exclaimed:

'Listen, Reeves. We'll never get anywhere with this bungler, who knows even less about bridges than I do. You're an engineer, aren't you? Well, you're going to take charge of the whole works and start off again right from the beginning, without bothering about what he says or does. First of all, find a proper position for it. Then we'll see . . .'

Reeves, delighted to be engaged once more on his pre-war occupation, had carefully studied the ground and sounded the depth of the river at various points. He had discovered an almost perfect bottom of hard sand which was quite capable of bearing the weight of a bridge.

Before Saito could find the right words to express his indignation, the Colonel had called on Reeves, who proceeded to state a few technical principles, then quoted certain pressure-and-soil resistance figures in tons per square inch which proved that the bridge would collapse under the weight of the trains if they insisted on building it over a swamp. When he had finished, the Colonel thanked him on behalf of all present and concluded:

'It seems quite clear, Colonel Saito, that we ought to shift the position of the bridge if we want to avoid disaster. May I ask your colleague for his advice on the matter?'

Saito swallowed his rage, sat down again and embarked on a heated discussion with his engineer. The Japanese had not been able to send their best technicians to Siam since they were needed for the war effort in the capital. This one, then, was not up to the mark. He was obviously lacking in experience, self-confidence and ability to command. He blushed when Colonel Nicholson drew his attention to Reeves's calculations, made a pretence of carefully studying them and finally, too nervous to be able to check them, and in a state of complete confusion, pathetically admitted that his colleague was right and that he himself had come to the same conclusion several days ago. It was such a shameful loss of face on the part of the Japanese that Saito went quite pale and drops of sweat broke out all over his contorted brow. He made a vague gesture of assent. The Colonel went on:

'So we're all agreed on this point, then, Colonel Saito? That means, all the work up to now has been useless. But it would have to be done all over again in any case, as there are serious faults in it.'

'Bad workmen,' snapped Saito, who was out for revenge. 'Japanese soldiers would have built those two sections of line in less than a fortnight.'

'Japanese soldiers would certainly have done better, because they're used to their officers commanding them. But I hope to show you the true worth of the British soldier quite soon, Colonel Saito. Incidentally, I ought to tell you that I've altered our men's quota.'

'Altered it!' Saito screamed.

'I've increased it,' the Colonel calmly replied, 'from one cubic yard to one and a half. It's in the general interest, and I felt this step would meet with your approval.'

The Japanese officer was completely dumbfounded, and the Colonel took advantage of this to put forward another question.

'You must realise, Colonel Saito, that we've got our own methods and I hope to prove their value, provided we're left free to apply them. We're fully aware that the success of this sort of venture depends more or less entirely on basic organisation. And while we're on the subject, here are my suggestions, which I should like to submit for your approval.'

At this point the Colonel outlined the administrative plan on which he had worked for the last two days with the help of his staff. It was a fairly simple one, designed to cope with this particular situation, in which each separate department had a proper function. Colonel Nicholson was to be in sole charge, and personally responsible for everyone to the Japanese. Captain Reeves was entrusted with the plans for all the preliminary, theoretical work, at the same time acting as technical adviser on the practical side. Major Hughes, who was good at handling men, was to be a sort of chief foreman, responsible for directing the labour. Immediately under him were the platoon officers, who were to supervise the individual working parties. An administrative department had also been formed, at the head of which the Colonel had appointed his best corporal clerk. His main duties were to be liaison, transmission of orders, control of the quota, distribution and maintenance of tools, etc.

'This department is absolutely essential,' the Colonel explained. 'I suggest, Colonel Saito, that you hold an inspection of the tools which were issued only a month ago. They're in a really scandalous state . . .'

'I strongly recommend that this scheme be accepted,' said Colonel Nicholson, as he looked up again after describing in detail the machinery for the new organisation and explaining the reasons which had led to its formation. 'I am, of course, at your disposal to enlighten you further on any point whenever you wish, and I assure you that any suggestion will be carefully studied. Do you agree in principle with these proposals?'

Saito was certainly in need of further explanation, but the Colonel had such a commanding presence as he pronounced these words that he could not refrain from making yet another gesture of assent. With a mere nod he agreed to the whole of this scheme, which deprived the Japanese of all initiative and rendered his own position more or less insignificant. He was prepared to put up with almost any humiliation. He was resigned to any sacrifice in order to see the piles ready to take the weight of this bridge, on which his very life depended. Reluctantly, in spite of himself, he felt confidence in the strange Western preparations for getting the work under way.

Encouraged by his initial success, Colonel Nicholson went on:

'There's another important point, Colonel Saito—the time factor. You realise, of course, how much extra work will be needed for the longer stretch of line. Then the new camp that will have to be built——'

'Why a new camp?' Saito protested. 'Surely the prisoners can march a couple of miles to their work!'

'My colleagues have studied the question from both angles,' Colonel Nicholson patiently replied. 'They have come to the conclusion . . .'

The calculations worked out by Reeves and Hughes showed quite clearly that the total number of hours spent on a daily march was far greater than the time needed to build a new camp. Once again Saito found himself out of his depth when confronted with conjectures based on wise Western forethought. The Colonel continued:

'Besides, we've already wasted over a month, as a result of an unfortunate disagreement for which we're not to blame. To get the bridge finished in the time laid down— and I promise you it will be if you accept my new suggestion—we'll have to start felling the trees and preparing the supports at once, while other teams simultaneously work on the railway line, and others still on the new camp.

According to Major Hughes's calculations—and he's had a great deal of labour experience—we shan't have enough men to get all this work done in time.'

Colonel Nicholson paused for a moment in the tense, expectant silence, then continued in a resolute tone:

'This is what I suggest, Colonel Saito. For the moment we'll put most of the British soldiers to work on the bridge. Only a small number will be available for the railway line, so I shall ask you to lend us your Japanese soldiers to reinforce this group, so as to get the first stretch finished as quickly as possible. I think it should also be up to your men to build up the new camp; they're more used to handling bamboo than mine are.'

It was at this particular moment that Clipton was swept away by one of his regular floods of affection. Until then he had felt several times like strangling the C.O. Now he could not stop looking at those blue eyes of his which, after glancing at the Japanese colonel, candidly interrogated every other member of the conference in turn, as though to demand an assurance that his last request was a fair one. He felt a momentary suspicion that there might be some cunning Machiavellian process at work behind that apparently artless exterior. Anxiously, earnestly, desperately, he examined each feature of that serene countenance in the wild hope of discovering some sign of treacherous underhand scheming. After a moment he gave up and looked away.

'It's out of the question,' he decided. 'Every word he said is meant sincerely. He really has tried to work out the best means of accelerating the work.'

He looked up again to watch Saito's face and derived much comfort from the sight. The Jap's features were the features of a victim on the rack, who had reached the limit of human endurance. He was tortured by shame and anger, yet caught in the trap of this relentlessly logical argument. He had little or no chance of getting out of it. Once again he was forced to yield, after hesitating between protest and submission. His only hope now was to regain a little of his authority while the work was actually in

progress. He was not yet aware of the abject state to which
he was to be reduced by the wisdom of the West. Clipton
knew that the Jap could never again retrieve the position
he had now abandoned.

Saito capitulated in his usual manner. He suddenly barked
out a few orders to his henchmen, speaking in Japanese.
Since the Colonel's speech had been so rapid that only he
had understood it, he was able to transmit the proposals
as his own idea and transform them into words of command. When he had finished, Colonel Nicholson brought
up one last point, a detail, but a tricky one, to which he
had had to give his full attention.

'We've still got to fix the quota for your men working
on the line, Colonel Saito. At first I thought of putting it at
one cubic yard so as not to overtire them, but don't you
think it would be best if we made it the same as the
British soldiers'? That would also create a healthy com-
petitive spirit . . .'

'The Japanese soldiers' quota will be *two* cubic yards,'
Saito burst out. 'I've already given the orders!'

Colonel Nicholson bowed in assent.

'In that case I expect we'll make good progress. I don't
think there's anything more to be said, Colonel Saito. It remains for me to thank you for your kind attention. If there
are no other questions, Gentlemen, I think we can declare
this meeting closed. We'll start work to-morrow on the
conditions to which we have agreed.'

He got up, saluted and withdrew, confident in the knowledge that he had conducted the meeting along the lines he
wanted, that common sense had won the day and that a
decisive step had been taken towards completing the bridge.
He had proved himself a skilful tactician and he knew that
he had deployed his forces in the best possible manner.
Clipton left with him, and together they walked back to
their hut.

'What fools they are, sir!' said the M.O., looking closely
at the Colonel. 'To think that, without us, they would have
built their bridge in a swamp and it would have capsized

under the weight of their trains loaded with troops and supplies!'

There was a strange glint in his eye as he spoke, but the Colonel's face remained inscrutable. This Sphinx-like character could not reveal his secret since he had no secret to reveal.

'Yes, aren't they?' he solemnly replied. 'They're what I've always said they were: primitive people, as undeveloped as children, who've acquired a veneer of civilisation too soon. Underneath it all they're absolutely ignorant. They can't do a thing by themselves. Without us, they'd still be living in the age of sailing ships and wouldn't own a single aircraft. Just children . . . yet so pretentious as well. Think of it, a work of this importance! As far as I can make out, they're only just capable of making a footbridge out of jungle creepers.'

IV

There is nothing in common between a bridge, as conceived by civilised society in the West, and the utilitarian scaffoldings which the Japanese forces were in the habit of erecting in the continent of Asia. There is likewise no similarity between the two respective methods of construction. Qualified technicians did exist in the Japanese Empire, but they had been kept behind in the capital. In the occupied territories construction work was the army's responsibility. The handful of engineers who had been despatched to Siam had little skill and even less authority, and for the most part were overruled by the professional soldiers.

The latter's method—which was speedy and, up to a point, fairly efficient—had been dictated by necessity; for during their advance through the countries they had overrun, they had found every installation destroyed by the enemy in retreat. It consisted of driving two rows of piles into the river-bed, then crowning these supports with a tangle of mixed timber hastily put together with no thought of plan or design and with a total disregard for the principle of static pressure, and finally adding extra bits of wood at any point which showed obvious signs of weakness.

On this uncouth superstructure, which sometimes reached an enormous height, thick beams were laid in two parallel rows; and on top of these, the only timber to be more or less properly shaped, went the rails themselves. The bridge was then considered to be finished. It fulfilled the need of the hour. There was no parapet, no footpath. The only way to walk across was to step from one beam to another, balancing above the chasm—a feat at which the Japanese were adept.

The first convoy would go jolting across at low speed. The engine sometimes came off the rails at the point where the bank met the bridge, but a gang of soldiers armed with crowbars usually managed to heave it upright again. The train would then move on. If the bridge was damaged at all more bits of timber would be added to the structure. And the next convoy would cross in the same way. The scaffolding would last a few days, a few weeks, sometimes even a few months, after which a flood would sweep it away, or else a series of more than usually violent jolts would make it capsize. Then the Japanese would patiently start rebuilding it. The materials they used were provided by the inexhaustible jungle.

The methods of Western civilisation, of course, are not so elementary. Captain Reeves represented an essential element of that civilisation—the mechanical—and would never have dreamed of being guided by such primitive empiricism.

But when it comes to bridge-building, Western mechanical procedure entails a lot of gruelling preliminaries, which swell and multiply the number of operations leading up to the actual construction. They entail, for instance, a detailed plan; and for this plan to be made it is essential to determine in advance the section and shape of every beam, the depth to which the piles are to be driven and a mass of other details. Now each section, each shape, and the depth entail further calculations, based on figures representing the resistance of the various materials to be used and the consistency of the ground. These figures in their turn, depend on co-efficients worked out according to 'standard patterns,' which in the civilised world are given in the form of mathematical tables. Mechanics, in fact, entail a complete *a priori* knowledge; and this mental creation, which precedes the material creation, is not the least important of the many achievements of Western genius.

There were no tables available on the banks of the Kwai, but Captain Reeves was an expert engineer and his theoretical knowledge enabled him to do without them, but only by increasing the number of preliminary duties and by experimenting with various weights and simple shapes before getting down to his calculations. He was thus enabled to determine his co-efficients by an easy method, using instruments hastily produced for the purpose, since there was not much time to spare.

With the approval of Colonel Nicholson, under the anxious eye of Saito and Clipton's sardonic gaze, he set to work on these tests. At the same time he traced the best possible course for the railway to take, and passed the result to Major Hughes for action. With this off his chest, and with all the necessary data for his calculations ready to hand, he embarked on the most interesting part of the work : the design and planning of the bridge.

He devoted himself to this task with the same professional conscientiousness that he had once shown when engaged on similar work for the Indian Government, and also with a passionate enthusiasm which he had hitherto tried to acquire, in vain, through reading suitable books (such as *The Bridge Builders*), but by which he was now suddenly carried away as a result of a casual remark passed by the C.O.

'You know, Reeves, I'm relying on you entirely. You're the only qualified man we have and I'm leaving everything in your hands. We've got to show we're superior to these savages. I realise how difficult it is in this God-forsaken place where you can't find what you need, but that makes the task all the more worth while.'

'You can count on me, sir,' Reeves had replied, feeling suddenly galvanised. 'I shan't let you down, and we'll show them what we're capable of doing.'

This was the chance he had been waiting for all his life. He had always dreamt of tackling a really big job without being badgered every other minute by administrative departments or maddened by interfering officials who ask ridiculous questions and try to put a spoke in the wheels, on the pretext of economy, thereby frustrating every creative effort. Here he was responsible to the Colonel and to no one else. The C.O. was favourably impressed; although he was a stickler for routine and 'proper channels,' he could at least see the other man's point of view and refused to be blinded by convention and protocol as far as the bridge was concerned. Besides, he had openly admitted he knew nothing about engineering, and made it quite clear he intended giving the junior officer his head. Certainly, the job was a difficult one, and there was a shortage of proper material, but Reeves promised to make up for every deficiency by his devotion to duty. He could already feel the breeze of creative inspiration fanning those hungry flames which overcome every obstacle in their path.

From that moment he did not allow himself a minute's leisure. He started by dashing off a sketch of the bridge, as he saw it in his mind's eye whenever he looked at the river, with its four majestic rows of piles meticulously in line, its bold but graceful superstructure towering a hundred feet above the water, its beams assembled according to a process he had himself invented and which he had tried in vain to make the conservative Government of India adopt years ago, its broad platform protected by a strong balustrade, allowing room not only for the railway itself but also for a vehicle track and footpath.

After that he set to work on the calculations and diagrams, and then on the actual design. He had managed to acquire a roll of fairly decent drawing-paper from his Japanese colleague, who kept sidling up behind him to gaze at the work in process with ill-concealed, bewildered admiration.

He fell into the habit of working like this from dawn till dusk, without a moment's rest, until he noticed that the hours of daylight were over all too soon, until he realised with dismay that the days were all too short and that his task would never be finished in the time he had allowed. And so, using Colonel Nicholson as his intermediary, he got permission from Saito to keep a lamp burning after Lights Out. From that day on, he spent every evening and sometimes half the night working on the design of the bridge. Sitting on a rickety footstool, using his wretched bamboo bed as a desk, with his drawing-paper spread out on a board which he had himself planed smooth with loving care, in the light of the tiny oil-lamp which filled the hut with fetid fumes, he would handle with expert ease the T- and set-square which he had taken such pains to make.

The only time these instruments were out of his fingers was when he seized a fresh sheet of paper and feverishly filled it with further calculations, sacrificing his sleep at the end of each tiring day in order to see his craftsmanship take shape in a masterpiece which was to prove the superiority of the West—this bridge which was to be used by the Japanese trains on their triumphant advance to the Bay of Bengal.

Clipton had at first believed that the preliminary stages in the Western *modus operandi* (the elaborate administrative plans, followed by painstaking research and mechanical tests) would retard the actual building of the bridge even more than the haphazard empiricism of the Japanese. It was not long before he realised how vain these hopes of his were and how wrong he had been to jeer at all the preparatory work undertaken during the long sleepless nights caused by Reeves's lamp. He began to understand that he had been a little too hasty in his criticism of the methods of Western civilisation on the day that Reeves submitted his finished plan to Major Hughes and the construction got under way with a speed surpassing even Saito's most optimistic dreams.

Reeves was not one of those people who becomes mes-

merised by symbolic preparations or who postpone taking
action indefinitely because they devote all their energies
to intellectual activity and think nothing of the practical
side. He kept one foot firmly on the ground. Besides, whenever he showed signs of pursuing theoretical perfection too
closely and shrouding the bridge in a fog of abstract figures,
Colonel Nicholson was there to guide his erring footsteps.
The Colonel had the practical sense of a born leader, who
never loses sight of his objective or the means at his disposal and who keeps his subordinates perfectly balanced
between idealism and reality.

He had consented to the preliminary tests on condition
that they were quickly completed. He had also approved
the blue-print and been given a detailed explanation of
the innovations due to Reeves's inventive genius. All he
had asked was that the latter should not overwork himself.

'We'll be getting along nicely, and then suddenly you'll
go sick, Reeves. The whole job depends on you, remember.'

So he began to watch Reeves carefully, and appealed to
common sense when he came to him one day with a worried look in his eye to inform him of certain particulars.

'There's one point that's bothering me, sir. I don't think
we should treat it too seriously, but I wanted to know
what you felt about it.'

'What is it, Reeves?' the Colonel asked.

'The wood's still damp, sir. We shouldn't be using
freshly-felled trees on a job like this. They should first be
left out in the open to dry.'

'How long would it take for these trees of yours to dry,
Reeves?'

'It all depends on what sort of wood it is, sir. With some
kinds it's advisable to wait eighteen months or even a
couple of years.'

'That's absolutely out of the question, Reeves,' the
Colonel protested, 'we've only got five months as it is.'

The Captain hung his head apologetically.

'Alas, sir, I realise that, and that's exactly what's worrying me.'

'And what's wrong with using fresh timber?'

'Some species contract, sir, and that might cause cracks and displacements once the work is under way. Not with every kind of wood, of course. Elm, for instance, hardly shifts at all. So naturally I've selected timber which is as much like elm as possible. The elm piles of London Bridge have lasted six hundred years, sir.'

'Six hundred years!' exclaimed the Colonel. There was a glint in his eye as he involuntarily turned towards the river. 'Six hundred years, Reeves, that would be a pretty good show!'

'Oh, but that's an exceptional case, sir. You could hardly count on more than fifty or sixty years in this place. Less, perhaps, if the timber dries out badly.'

'We'll just have to take that chance, Reeves,' the Colonel firmly decided. 'You must use fresh timber. We can't achieve the impossible. If they blame us for any fault in the construction, at least we'll be able to tell them that it couldn't be avoided.'

'Right, sir. Just another question. Creosote, for protecting the beams against insect damage . . . I think we'll have to do without it, sir. The Japs haven't got any. Of course, we could make a substitute . . . I'd thought of setting up a wood-alcohol still. That might do, but it would take some time . . . No, on second thoughts, I don't think we'd better . . .'

'Why not, Reeves?' asked the Colonel, who was fascinated by all these technical details.

'Well, there's a difference of opinion on this, sir; but the best authorities advise against creosoting when the timber's not sufficiently dry. It keeps the sap and the damp in, sir; and then there's a risk of rot setting in at once.'

'In that case we'll have to do without creosote, Reeves. You must bear in mind that we can't afford to embark on any scheme beyond our means. Don't forget the bridge has an immediate role to fulfil.'

'Apart from those two snags, sir, I'm quite certain we can build a bridge here which will be perfectly all right from the technical point of view and reasonably strong.'

'That's it, Reeves. You're on the right track. A reason-

ably strong bridge which is all right from the technical
point of view. A bridge, in fact, and not a Heath Robinson
contraption. That's what we want. As I've said before, I'm
relying on you entirely.'

Colonel Nicholson left his technical adviser, feeling
pleased with the simple phrase he had coined to define his
objective.

V

Shears—or 'Number One' as he was called by the Siamese
partisans in the remote hamlet where the envoys of Force
316 were now in hiding—was likewise the sort of man
who devotes a great deal of thought and care to systematic
preparation. In fact the high regard in which he was held
at Headquarters was as much due to the caution and
patience he showed before taking any action as to his
cheerfulness and determination when the time for action
arrived. Warden, Professor Warden, his second-in-com-
mand, also had a well-earned reputation for leaving nothing to chance unless circumstances dictated otherwise. As
for Joyce, the third and youngest member of the team, who
was still fresh from the course he had been on at the Plastic
and Destructions Company's special school at Calcutta, he
seemed to have his head screwed on the right way, in spite
of his youth, and Shears valued his opinion. And so, during
the daily conferences held in the two-room native hut
which had been put at their disposal, any promising idea
was carefully considered and every suggestion thoroughly
examined.

One evening the three of them were studying a map
which Joyce had just pinned up on the bamboo wall.

'Here's the approximate course of the railway, sir,' he
said. 'The reports seem to tally pretty well.'

Joyce, who was an industrial designer in civilian life, had
been detailed to keep a large-scale map marked with all the
intelligence available on the Burma-Siam railway.

There was plenty of information. During the month since they had safely landed on their selected dropping-zone they had succeeded in winning the friendship of the local population over quite a wide area. They had been received by the Siamese agents, and been housed in this little hamlet inhabited by hunters and smugglers and hidden away in the corner of the jungle well away from the nearest line of communication. The natives hated the Japanese. Shears, who was trained to take nothing for granted, had gradually been convinced of the loyalty of his hosts.

The first part of their mission was successfully under way. They had secretly established contact with several village headmen. Volunteers were ready to rally round them. The three officers had started instructing them and were now training them in the use of the weapons employed by Force 316. The most important of these was 'plastic,' a soft brown paste as malleable as clay, in which several generations of chemists in the Western world had patiently contrived to amalgamate the best features of every known explosive and several others besides.

'There are any amount of bridges, sir,' Joyce went on, 'but if you ask me, most of them aren't up to much. Here's the list, from Bangkok right up to Rangoon. complete as far as our information goes.

The 'sir' was for the benefit of Major Shears, his 'Number One.' Although discipline was strict in Force 316, such formality was nevertheless not usual among members of a special mission; and Shears had asked Joyce several times to stop calling him 'sir.' He had not been able to break him of the habit—a pre-war habit, Shears imagined, which made the young man cling to this mode of address.

Yet so far Shears could find nothing but praise for Joyce, whom he had selected from the Calcutta school on the instructors' reports as well as on the candidate's physical appearance, but most of all on his own instinctive judgment.

The reports were good and the comments flattering. Young Joyce, it seemed, who was a volunteer like all the other members of Force 316, had always given complete satisfaction and had shown exceptional keenness on every part of the course—which was something to be said for him, in Shears's opinion. According to his personal file, he had been a draughtsman on the staff of a big industrial and commercial concern—probably only a minor employee. But Shears had not enquired any further. He felt there was no profession that could not eventually lead to the Plastic and Destructions Company, Ltd., and that a man's pre-war career was his own business.

On the other hand, all Joyce's visible qualities would not have been sufficient to warrant Shears's taking him in as the third member of the team, if they had not been backed up by others which were less easy to define and for which he relied on little else but his own personal impression. He had known volunteers who were excellent during training, but whose nerve failed them when it came to certain duties demanded by Force 316. He did not hold this against them. Shears had his own ideas on this subject.

He had therefore sent for this future companion of his in order to try and find out what sort of a man he was. He had asked his friend Warden to be present at the interview, for the Professor's advice in a selection of this sort was always worth considering. He had been favourably impressed by Joyce's appearance. His physical strength was probably not much above the average, but he was fit and seemed a well-balanced type. His clear, frank answers to the questions he was asked showed he had a practical mind, that he never lost sight of his objective and was well aware of what he was letting himself in for. Apart from this, his keenness showed unmistakably in his eyes. He was obviously dying to accompany the two veterans ever since he had heard the rumours of a dangerous mission being planned.

Shears had then brought up a point which he considered important, as indeed it was.

'Do you think you'd be capable of using a weapon like this?' he had asked.

He had shown him a razor-sharp dagger. This knife was part of the kit which members of Force 316 took in with them on every special mission. Joyce had not batted an eye-

lid. He had replied that he had been taught how to handle
the weapon and that the course included practising with it
on dummies. Shears had repeated the question.

'That's not exactly what I meant. What I want to know
is: are you quite sure that you'd be really "capable" of
using it in cold blood? Lots of men know how to use it,
but aren't able to when it comes to the point.'

Joyce had understood. He had silently thought the matter
over, then solemnly replied:

'That's a question I've often asked myself, sir.'

'A question you've often asked yourself?' Shears had
repeated, looking at him closely.

'Yes, sir, really. And I must admit, it's worried me quite
a lot. I've tried to imagine myself——'

'And what was the answer?'

Joyce had hesitated, but only for a second.

'Speaking quite frankly, sir, I don't think I'd disappoint
you if it ever came to the point. I don't honestly. But I
couldn't say for certain. I'd do my very best, sir.'

'You've never had a chance of using one of these in
anger, is that it?'

'That's it, sir. My job never called for that sort of thing,'
Joyce had replied, as though offering an apology.

He seemed to be so genuinely sorry about it that Shears
could not help smiling. Warden had immediately joined
the conversation:

'I say, Shears, this chap seems to think that my old job,
for instance, is a special qualification for this of work. A
professor of Oriental languages! And what about you—a
cavalry officer!'

'I didn't mean that exactly, sir,' Joyce had stammered in
his embarrassment.

'Ours is the only firm I know,' Shears had philosophically
concluded, 'in which you'd find, as you say, an Oxford
graduate and an ex-cavalryman doing this particular sort
of work—so why not an industrial designer as well?'

'Take him,' was all that Warden said when asked for
his advice as soon as the interview was over. Shears had
done so. Thinking it over, he had been fairly pleased with

the candidate's answers. He was just as suspicious of men who overestimated themselves as of those who under-estimated. The sort he liked were those who were capable of distinguishing the tricky part of a mission in advance, who had sufficient foresight to prepare for it and enough imagination to see it quite clearly in their mind's eye—so long as they did not let it become an obsession. So from the start he had been satisfied with his team. As for Warden, he had known him for a long time and knew exactly how far he was 'capable.'

They pored over the map for some time, while Joyce pointed out the bridges and described the particular features of each. Shears and Warden listened carefully, with curi-ously tense expressions, although they already knew the subaltern's report by heart. Bridges always provoked a passionate interest in every member of the Plastic and De-structions Co., an interest of an almost mystical nature.

'These are just footbridges you're describing, Joyce,' said Shears. 'Don't forget, we want a really worth-while target.'

'I only mentioned them, sir, in order to refresh my memory. As far as I can see, there are only three worth bothering about.'

Every bridge was not equally attractive to Force 316. Number One agreed with Colonel Green that they should not put the Japs on their guard before the railway was completed by attacking relatively unimportant targets. He had therefore decided that the team should lie low in the hide-out for the time being and do no more than collate and co-ordinate the information of the native agents.

'It would be silly to spoil the whole show by blowing up a few trucks just for the fun of the thing,' he would some-times say in order to curb his companions' impatience. 'We want to start off in a really big way. That will enhance our reputation in the country and make the Siamese look up to us. Let's wait till the trains start running.'

Since his firm intention was to start off 'in a big way,' it was clear that the less important bridges had to be ex-cluded. The result of the initial blow was to compensate for

the long period of activity and preparation and to endow the
mission, in his own eyes at least, with an aura of success,
even if circumstances dictated that nothing else should
come of it. Shears knew that one could never be certain of
a first attack being followed up by a second. He kept this
to himself, but his two companions had realised the reasons for his plan, and the discovery of this ulterior motive
had not worried the ex-professor Warden whose rational
mind approved of such methods of seeing and foreseeing.

It had not seemed to worry Joyce either, nor had it
dampened the enthusiasm he had felt at the prospect of a
worth-while attack. On the contrary, it seemed to have
spurred him on to greater efforts and made him concentrate
all his youthful powers on this probably unique opportunity, on this unhoped for target suddenly flashing in front
of him like a lighthouse, casting its brilliant beams of success on to the past for all eternity, lighting up with its
magic flames the grey gloom which had so far dimmed his
path.

'Joyce is right,' said Warden, as sparing as ever in his
speech. 'There are only three worth-while bridges. One of
them is Camp Three's.'

'We'll have to give that one up, I'm afraid,' said Shears.
'The open ground doesn't lend itself to attack. Apart from
that, it's in flat country. The banks are low. It would be
too easy to repair.'

'The other one's near Camp Ten.'

'It's worth considering. But it happens to be in Burma,
where we haven't the support of the native partisans.
Besides . . .'

'The third one sir,' Joyce suddenly said, without realising he was butting in to his C.O.'s conversation, 'the third
one's the bridge on the River Kwai. It hasn't any of those
drawbacks. The river's four hundred feet across, with steep,
high banks on both sides. It's only two or three days' march
from here. The area's practically uninhabited and covered in
jungle. We could approach it without being observed and
command it from a hill from which the whole valley's vis-

ible. It's a long way from the nearest large town. The Japs are taking special care over its construction. It's bigger than all the other bridges and has four rows of piles. It's the most important job on the whole line, and the best placed one.'

'You seem to have studied the agents' reports pretty thoroughly,' observed Shears.

'They're quite clear, sir. It seems to me that this bridge . . .'

'I can see that the Kwai bridge is worth considering,' said Shears, as he leant over the map. 'Your judgment's not so dusty for a beginner. Colonel Green and I had already noted that particular crossing. But our information's not yet sufficiently complete; and there may be other bridges which could be more easily attacked. And how far has the work progressed on this wonderful bridge, Joyce, which you talk of as though you had actually seen it?'

VI

The work was well under way. The British soldier is by nature hard working and puts up with strict discipline without a murmur provided he has confidence in his officers and starts the day off with the prospect of unlimited physical exercise to counteract any nervous tension. The soldiers in the River Kwai camp had a high opinion of Colonel Nicholson—and who would not have after his heroic resistance? Besides, the sort of work they were doing did not involve much thought. So after a short period of indecision, during which they tried to get to the bottom of the C.O.'s real intentions, they had set to work with a will, eager to show their skill as builders now that they had proved their cunning as saboteurs. In any case Colonel Nicholson had taken steps to avoid any chance of misunderstanding, first by delivering an address in which he explained quite clearly what was expected of them, and secondly by inflicting severe punishments on a few recalcitrants who had not fully understood. This action had seemed so well intended that the victims did not hold it against him.

'Believe me, I know these fellows better than you do,' was the Colonel's retort to Clipton, who had dared to protest against the set task, which he considered too heavy for men who were undernourished and in a poor state of health. 'It's taken me thirty years to get to know them. Nothing's worse for morale than inactivity, and their physical welfare depends largely on their morale. Troops who are bored, Clipton, are troops doomed in advance to defeat. Let them get slack and you'll see an unhealthy spirit developing in the unit. But fill every minute of their day with hard work, and cheerfulness and health are guaranteed.'

'Be happy in your work!' murmured Clipton disloyally. 'That was General Yamashita's motto.'

'And it's not such a bad one, Clipton. We shouldn't hesitate to adopt a principle of the enemy's if it happens to be a good one. If there wasn't any work for them to do, I'd invent some for them. As it is, we've got the bridge.'

Clipton could find no words to express what he felt and could only sullenly repeat:

'Yes, we've got the bridge all right.'

In any case the British soldiers had already revolted on their own against an attitude and code of behaviour which clashed with their instinctive urge to do a job properly. Even before the Colonel intervened, subversive activity had become for most of them a distasteful duty, and some of them had not waited for his orders before using their muscles and tools to proper purpose. It was their natural reaction, as Westerners, to make a loyal and considerable effort in return for their daily bread, and their Anglo-Saxon blood encouraged them to concentrate this effort on something solid and constructive. The Colonel had not been wrong about them. His new régime led to a rise in morale.

Since the Japanese soldier is equally well disciplined and hard working, and since Saito had threatened to string his men up if they failed to prove themselves better workers than the British, the two stretches of line had been quickly completed, while the huts for the new camp had been erected and made habitable. At about the same time Reeves had put the finishing touches to his plans and passed them to Major Hughes, who was thus drawn into the scheme and given a chance to show what he was worth. Thanks to his organising ability, his knowledge of the troops and his experience of how man-power can be most effectively employed, the labour under his direction achieved tangible results from the very start.

The first thing Hughes did was to divide the personnel into different groups and allot a specific task to each, so that while one was occupied on cutting down trees, another would be trimming the trunks, a third making the beams, while the largest of all was engaged on pile-driving, and many more besides were employed on the superstructure and platform. Some of the teams—not the least important ones, in Hughes's opinion—were made up of various experts in such tasks as the erection of the scaffolding, the transport of the materials and the maintenance of the tools: tasks of secondary importance to the actual construction work, but to which Western foresight devotes—and not without reason—as much care as to the immediately productive work.

This division of labour was a wise move and proved most effective, as it always does when not carried to extremes. As soon as a stack of planks was ready, and the first scaffoldings were in position, Hughes set his team of pile-drivers to work. Theirs was an arduous task, the hardest and most thankless of the whole undertaking. In the absence of all mechanical labour, these new bridge-builders were reduced to using the same methods as the Japanese, that is to say they were obliged to drop a heavy weight on to the head of each pile and repeat this operation until it was firmly embedded in the river. The 'ram,' which dropped from a height of eight or ten feet, had to be re-hoisted each time by a system of ropes and pulleys, then allowed to fall once more over and over again. At each blow the pile would sink an infinitesimal fraction of an inch, for the ground was as hard as rock. It was unrewarding, soul-destroying work. There was no visible sign of progress from one minute to the next, and the sight of a group of more or less naked men tugging at a rope reminded one gloomily of a slave-gang. Hughes had put one of the best subalterns in command of this team—Harper, a man with plenty of drive, who urged the prisoners on better than anyone else by shouting out the time in a booming voice. Thanks to his encouragement, this punishing task was accomplished with zeal and cheerfulness. Under the astonished eyes of the Japanese the four parallel rows gradually crept forward across the water towards the left bank.

At one moment Clipton had almost expected the embedding of the first pile to be celebrated by some solemn ritual, but there had only been a few simple formalities. Colonel Nicholson had confined himself to seizing the rope of the ram and tugging manfully, to set an example, for as long as it took to come down a dozen times.

Once the pile-drivers were well under way, Hughes launched the teams engaged on the superstructure. They in their turn were followed by others employed on laying down the platform with its broad tracks and parapets. The various activities had been so well co-ordinated that from then on work went forward with mathematical regularity.

An observer, blind to elementary detail but keen on general principles, might have regarded the development of the bridge as an uninterrupted process of natural growth. That was certainly the impression that Colonel Nicholson had of it. With a satisfied eye he witnessed this gradual materialisation, without connecting it in any way with humble human activity. Consequently he saw it only as something abstract and complete in itself: a living symbol of the fierce struggles and countless experiments by which a nation gradually raises itself in the course of centuries to a state of civilisation.

It was in much the same light that the bridge sometimes appeared also to Reeves. He gazed at it in wonder as it simultaneously rose above the water and stretched across the river, reaching its maximum width almost at once, majestically registering in all three dimensions the palpable shape of creation at the foot of these wild Siamese mountains, representing in miraculously concrete form the wealth of fruitful imagination and labour.

Saito too was overwhelmed by the magic of this daily prodigy. In spite of all his efforts, he could not altogether conceal his astonishment and admiration. His surprise was only to be expected. Since he had not fully understood, and had certainly never analysed, the subtler aspects of Western civilisation—as Colonel Nicholson so rightly observed—he could not realise to what extent method, organisation, calculation, theoretical planning and expert co-ordination of human activities facilitate and eventually accelerate any practical undertaking. The purpose and usefulness of this sort of intellectual groundwork will always be beyond the comprehension of savages.

As for Clipton, he was definitely convinced of his initial stupidity and humbly recognised the folly of the sarcastic attitude he had shown towards the application of modern industrial methods to the construction of the River Kwai bridge.

He inwardly apologised for this, showing a characteristic sense of fair-mindedness mingled with remorse for having been so short-sighted. He was forced to admit that the methods of the Western world had in this case led to positive results. Starting from this premise, he pursued the argument a stage further and came to the conclusion that such 'methods' are invariably effective and invariably produce 'results.' Those who set themselves up as critics of these methods never give them a fair trial. He himself, like so many others, had given way to the temptation of a cheap sneer.

The bridge, growing daily larger and more beautiful, soon reached the middle of the river, then went past it. At this stage it became quite obvious to everyone that it would be finished before the date laid down by the Japanese High Command and would cause no delay to the triumphant advance of the victorious army.

PART THREE

I

Joyce swallowed the drink he had been given in one gulp. His arduous expedition had not told on him. He was still quite fresh and there was a sparkle in his eye. Before he had even taken off the outlandish Siamese disguise, in which Shears and Warden could scarcely recognise him, he insisted on reporting the main events of his mission.

'It's worth having a go at it, sir, I'm certain. It won't be easy—let's face it—but it's possible and definitely worth while. There's thick jungle. The river's a broad one. The bridge runs across a gully. The banks are steep. The train couldn't be cleared, except with a great deal of equipment.'

'Begin at the beginning,' said Shears. 'Or do you want to have a shower first?'

'I'm not tired, sir.'

'Give him a chance,' growled Warden. 'Can't you see he wants to talk, not rest?'

Shears smiled. It was obvious that Joyce was just as eager to make his report as he himself was to hear it. They settled down as comfortably as possible in front of the map. With characteristic foresight Warden handed Joyce a second glass. In the room next door the two Siamese partisans who had acted as the young man's guide were squatting on the floor, surrounded by some of the local villagers. They had already begun to describe their expedition and made flattering references to the behaviour of the white man whom they had accompanied.

'It's been quite a stiff march, sir,' Joyce began. 'Three nights through the jungle, and hard going all the way. But the partisans were splendid. They kept their promise and took me to the top of the hill on the left bank, which commands the whole valley, the camp and the bridge. A perfect O.P.'

'I hope no one saw you?'

'Not a chance, sir. We only moved at night, and it was so dark I had to keep one hand on the shoulder of the chap in front. We lay up during the day in the undergrowth, which was thick enough to discourage any prying eyes. But in any case it's such wild country, even that wasn't necessary. We didn't see a soul till we arrived.'

'Good,' said Shears. 'Go on.'

As he listened, Number One surreptitiously scrutinised Joyce to see if the opinion he was beginning to form of him was justified. To him the values of this reconnaissance were two-fold; it gave him a chance of assessing the young man's abilities when left to his own devices. The first impression he made on his return was favourable. The cheerful appearance of the two natives was another good sign. Shears knew that imponderables like these should not be disregarded. Joyce was certainly a little over-excited not only by what he had seen but also by the change in atmosphere, by the comparative peace of these quarters after the countless hazards to which he had been exposed since his departure.

'The Siamese weren't far wrong, sir. It's a really beautiful job.'

Zero hour drew nearer and nearer as the rails stretched further and further along the embankment at the cost of countless hardships suffered by the Allied prisoners of war in Burma and Siam. Shears and his two companions had followed the daily progress of the line. Joyce spent hours emending his map and keeping it up to date according to the latest information received. Every week he added to the line in red pencil which represented each newly-completed section. The line was now almost unbroken from Bangkok to Rangoon. The more important river crossings were indicated by a cross. The particulars of each construction were noted down on slips of paper, carefully kept up to date by Warden, who liked to have everything neat and tidy.

With their information on the line growing more complete and more accurate, their attention was irresistibly drawn to the River Kwai bridge, which had attracted them right from the start by its many advantages. With their specialised knowledge of bridges, they had been amazed by the exceptional number of circumstances favourable to the plan which they had instinctively started to work out, a plan which combined the practical sense and the imagination typical of the Plastic and Destructions Co., Ltd. Prompted by instinct as much as by logic, they had gradually come to pin all their faith and hopes on the River Kwai bridge and on nothing else. They had considered a number of other bridges just as carefully and had discussed their respective advantages, but had ended up by choosing this one, which seemed naturally and purposely designed for them as an operational target. The 'big show,' which was at first no more than a vague, abstract idea existing only in the imagination, was now represented by a concrete body in time and space—a vulnerable target, in other words, liable to every contingency, to every degradation of which the mind of man is capable, and especially liable to annihilation.

'This isn't a job for the R.A.F.,' Shears had observed. 'It's not easy to destroy a wooden bridge from the air. If the bombs find their mark only two or three arches are damaged. The rest are just knocked about a bit. The Japs can patch it up in no time, they're past-masters at that sort of thing. Whereas we can not only blow the whole thing sky-high and shatter the piles at water-level, but also time the explosion for when a train is actually crossing the bridge. Then the whole convoy'll come crashing down into the river, increasing the damage and putting every beam out of action. I've seen it happen before. Traffic was held up for weeks. And that was in a civilised part of the world where the enemy was able to bring up cranes. Here they'll have to make a detour in the line and build the bridge all over again—not to mention the loss of a train and its load of war material. What a show! I can just see it . . .'

All three could imagine what a show it would be. The

attack had assumed concrete shape over which the imagination could wander at will. A succession of mental snapshots, some of them underexposed, others in bright technicolour, disturbed Joyce's sleep. The former appertained to the period of clandestine preparation, the latter culminated in such a brilliant picture that the smallest detail stood out amazingly sharp and clear: the train poised above the gully, with the River Kwai sparkling underneath between two blocks of jungle. His own hand was clutching the plunger. His eyes were fixed on a certain point in the centre of the bridge. The distance between that point and the engine was rapidly decreasing. He had to push the plunger down at the right moment. The distance between them was now only a few feet, only one foot. At that very moment he automatically pushed down the plunger. On the bridge which he saw in his dreams, he had already reconnoitred and found a suitable spot, exactly half-way across!

One day he had anxiously exclaimed: 'I only hope the Air Force chaps won't have a go at it, sir, before we do.'

'I've already sent a message to tell them to keep out of it,' Shears had answered. 'I don't think we'll be worried by them.'

During this period of inactivity countless reports had come in, all referring to the bridge which the partisans were keeping under observation from the top of a nearby hill. They themselves had not yet approached it in case the locals got wind of the presence of white men in the area. They had had it described to them hundreds of times, and the more intelligent agents had even made a drawing of it in the sand. From their hide-out they had followed every stage in its construction, and were amazed by the unusual method and system which seemed to govern each successive phase and which were confirmed by every report. They were used to sifting the truth from any rumour, and had quickly detected a feeling akin to admiration in the partisans' description of the bridge. The Siamese were not qualified to appreciate the technical genius of Captain Reeves, nor the organisation for which Colonel Nicholson was responsible, but they were fully aware that this was no shapeless scaffolding in the usual Japanese style. Primitive people have an instinctive appreciation of applied art and design.

'God Almighty!' Shears would sometimes cry out in desperation. 'If what our chaps say is true, it's a second George Washington Bridge they're building. They're trying to compete with the Yanks!'

Such unusually lavish work, amounting almost to extravagance—for according to the Siamese, there was a road running alongside the line, which was wide enough for two trucks abreast—was an intriguing but disturbing prospect. An installation of this size would almost certainly be more closely guarded than ever. On the other hand, it might be of even greater strategic importance than he had thought, so that attacking it would be all the more worth while.

The natives had quite a lot to say about the prisoners. They had seen them working almost naked in the scorching sun, working without a break and under strict surveillance. When they heard this, all three of them forgot about their scheme and gave a moment's thought to their wretched fellow-countrymen. Knowing the Japs as they did, they could well imagine how far their brutality would go in order to get a job like this one finished.

'If only they knew we were in the offing, sir,' Joyce had said one day. 'If only they knew this bridge of theirs was never going to be used, it might raise their morale a bit.'

'Perhaps,' Shears had answered, 'but we can't afford to contact them. That's out of the question, Joyce. In our job security's the first essential, even among friends. They'd let their imagination run riot. They'd start trying to help us and might give the whole show away by having a go at the bridge themselves. The Japs would get wind of it, and the only result would be terrible reprisals. No, they've got to be kept out of it. We mustn't allow the Japs even to think of the possibility of the prisoners' co-operating with us.'

One day Shears had suddenly decided to test the reliability of the fabulous reports which were coming in every day from the River Kwai.

'One of us will have to go and have a look. The work will be finished any day now, and we can't go on relying on these chaps' reports, which seem utterly fantastic. You'd better go, Joyce. I want to know what this bridge is really like, understand? How big is it? How many piles are there? I want the exact figures. How can it be approached? How is it guarded? What are the chances of attacking it? Do what you can, but keep your head down. You mustn't let yourself be seen at any price, bear that in mind. But for God's sake get me some proper information on this bridge!'

II

'I saw it through my glasses, sir, as clearly as I can see you now.'

'Begin from the beginning,' Shears insisted in spite of his impatience. 'How did it go?'

Joyce had set off one night accompanied by two natives who were accustomed to these secret nocturnal expeditions since it was their practice to smuggle wads of opium and cases of cigarettes over the border between Burma and Siam. They claimed that the paths they used were quite safe; but it was so important for no one to know that a European was in the neighbourhood that Joyce had insisted on disguising himself as a Siamese peasant and on dyeing his skin with a brown pigment made up in Calcutta for just such an occasion.

He soon saw that his guides had been telling the truth. The real enemies in this jungle were the mosquitoes and particularly the leeches, which fastened on to his bare legs and climbed up his body; he could feel them sticking to him each time he stroked his skin. He had done his best to overcome his disgust and to disregard them. He had almost succeeded. In any case he could not get rid of them during the night. He refrained from lighting a cigarette in order to burn them off, and he needed all his wits about him to keep up with the Siamese.

'Tough going?'

'Fairly tough, sir. As I said, I had to keep one hand on the shoulder of the chap in front. And these fellows' so-called paths have to be seen to be believed!'

For three nights they had made him clamber up hill and down dale. They followed rocky river-beds blocked here and there with stinking clumps of rotting vegetation, and each time they brushed against these they collected a rich crop of fresh leeches. His guides showed a preference for these paths, in which they were sure they could not get lost. They kept going till dawn. When the first rays of the sun appeared they dived into the undergrowth and quickly ate the boiled rice and cooked meat they had brought for the journey. The two Siamese then squatted under a tree until nightfall, puffing away at a bubbling water-pipe which they always carried with them. That was their method of relaxing after the rigours of the night. From time to time they dropped off between two puffs, without even shifting their position.

Joyce, however, insisted on sleeping properly in order to harvest his strength, for he was anxious to make the best of every circumstance on which the success of his mission depended. He began by getting rid of the leeches which covered his body. Some of them, completely glutted, had fallen off by themselves during the night, leaving a little clot of congealed blood. The others, which had not yet had their fill, stuck firmly to this prey of theirs which the fortunes of war had brought into the jungles of Siam. Under the glow of a burning cigarette their swollen bodies contracted, twisted, then finally let go and fell on the ground, where he squashed them between two stones. Then he lay down on a ground-sheet and went to sleep at once; but the ants did not leave him in peace for long.

Attracted by the drops of congealed blood which bespattered his skin, they took this opportunity to advance in long black and red cohorts. He learnt to distinguish between the two as soon as he felt them, without even opening his eyes. Against the red ones there was nothing he could do. Their sting was like white-hot pincers on his sores. A single one was unbearable; and they advanced in battalions. He was forced to yield ground and find some other spot where he could lie down until they located him again and launched a fresh attack. The black ones, especially the large black ones, were not so bad. They did not sting and their tickling did not wake him up until his sores were alive with them.

Yet he always managed to get enough sleep, quite enough to have enabled him, when night fell again, to scale mountains ten times as high and a hundred times as steep as the hills of Siam. He felt drunk with delight at being on his own during this reconnaissance, which was the first stage in the development of the big attack. It was on his own energy, his own judgment, on his own decisions during this expedition that the success of the operation depended—of this he was certain—and the certainty enabled him to preserve intact his inexhaustible reserves of strength. He kept his eyes firmly fixed on the imaginary bridge, that shadowy form which was a permanent part of his dream-world. The mere thought of it endowed his every gesture with an unlimited magic power which increased his glorious chances of success.

The actual bridge, the bridge on the River Kwai, had suddenly sprung into view when, after a final climb, the stiffest they had so far encountered, they reached the top of a hill commanding the valley. They had kept moving later than on the previous nights, and the sun had already risen by the time they reached the observation post which the Siamese had mentioned in their reports. He looked down at the bridge as though from an aeroplane. Several hundred feet below him a light-coloured band stretched across the water between two strips of jungle; a small gap over on the right enabled him to make out the geometric network of piles and platform. For some time he noticed no other feature of the panorama unrolled at his feet, neither the

camp directly opposite him on the far bank, nor even the
groups of prisoners at work on the construction itself. It
was an ideal O.P. and he felt perfectly safe. The Japanese
patrols were hardly likely to risk their necks in the undergrowth between him and the river.

'I saw it as plainly as I can see you now, sir. The Siamese
had not exaggerated. It's a big job. It's properly built. It's
nothing like any other Japanese bridge. Here are a few
sketches, for what they're worth.'

He had recognised it at once. The shock of confronting
this materialised ghost of his was not due to surprise but,
on the contrary, to its familiar aspect. The bridge was
exactly as he had imagined it. He studied it, anxiously at
first, then with overpowering relief. The general background also conformed to the patiently worked-out pattern
of his imagination and hopes. It differed only in detail. The
water did not sparkle as he had seen it in his mind's eye.
It was muddy. For a moment he felt almost cheated, but
cheered up at the thought that this defect would better
serve their purpose.

For two days he lay concealed, crouching in the undergrowth, eagerly observing the bridge through his binoculars
and studying the ground over which the attack was to be
launched. He had painted a mental picture of the general
lay-out and individual features, taking notes and making a
rough sketch of the paths, the camp, the Japanese huts, the
bends in the river and even of the large rocks protruding
here and there out of the water.

'The current's not very strong, sir. The river's an easy
proposition for a small boat or a good swimmer. The
water's muddy. There's a motor-road over the bridge, and
four rows of piles. I saw the prisoners driving them in with
a ram—the British prisoners. They've almost reached the
left bank, sir, the bank with the O.P. on it. Other teams
are following up behind. The bridge'll be ready in a month,
I should think. The superstructure . . .'

He now had such a mass of information to report that he
could not keep it in its proper order. Shears let him run on

without interrupting him. There would be time enough, when he had finished speaking, to question him on specific points.

'The superstructure's a geometric network of cross-beams which looks as if it's been carefully designed. The supports are all squared up and properly put together. I could see the joints in detail through my glasses. A really well-designed job, sir, and a solid one, too, let's face it. It'll mean more than just smashing up a few bits of wood. While I was there, sir, I thought of the safest way of dealing with it, and I think it's the simplest as well. I think we'll have to go for the piles in the water, or rather under the water. It's thick with sediment. The charges won't be noticed. That way the whole works will capsize all together.'

'Four rows of piles,' Shears muttered. 'That's a big job, you know. Why the hell couldn't they build this bridge of theirs like all the other ones?'

'How far apart are the piles in each row?' asked Warden, who liked to have exact figures.

'Ten feet.'

Shears and Warden silently made a mental calculation.

'We'll have to allow for a length of sixty feet, to be on the safe side,' Warden finally observed. 'That makes six piles per row, in other words twenty-four to "prepare." It'll take some time.'

'We could do it in a night, sir, I'm certain. Once we're under the bridge there's nothing to worry about. It's wide enough to give ample cover. The water washing up against the piles muffles any other sound. I know——'

'How do you know what it's like under the bridge?' Shears asked, gazing at him with renewed interest.

'Just a moment, sir. I haven't told you the whole story. I went and had a look myself.'

'You went underneath it?'

'I had to, sir. You told me not to get too close, but that was the only way I could get the information I wanted. I climbed down from the O.P., on the blind side of the hill from the river. I felt I couldn't let this opportunity slip through my fingers, sir. The Siamese took me along some wild-boar tracks. . . . We had to move on all fours.[1]

'How long did it take you?'

'About three hours, sir. We set off in the evening. I wanted to be in position by nightfall. It was a risk, of course, but I wanted to see for myself . . .[1]

'It's sometimes not such a bad idea to put your own interpretation on the orders you're given,' said Number One, as he glanced across at Warden. 'You got there, anyway—that's the main thing.'

'No one saw me, sir. We fetched up on the river about a quarter of a mile upstream from the bridge. Unfortunately there's a small native village tucked away there; but everyone was asleep. I sent the guides back. I wanted to reconnoitre on my own. I slipped into the water and floated down with the current.[1]

'Was it a clear night?' asked Warren.

'Fairly. No moon; but no clouds either. The bridge is pretty high, they can't see a thing . . .'

'Let's get things in their proper order,' said Shears. 'How did you approach the bridge?'[1]

'I floated down on my back, sir, completely submerged except for my mouth. Above me . . .[1]

'Damn it all, Shears,' growled Warden, 'you might think of me when a mission like this crops up again.'

'I'll probably think of myself first if there ever is another one,' Shears replied.

Joyce described the scene so vividly that his two companions succumbed to his own enthusiasm and felt really disappointed that they had missed this part of the fun.

It was on the very day that he reached the O.P. after three nights' exhausting march that he had suddenly decided to do the reconnaissance. He had not been able to wait a moment longer. After seeing the bridge almost within arm's reach, he felt he simply had to go and touch it with his hand.

Flat on his back in the water, unable to make out a single detail in the solid mass of the banks, barely conscious of being carried downstream and unaware of the current, his only landmark was the long horizontal outline of the bridge. It stood out black against the sky. It grew larger as he approached it, soaring up into the heavens, while the stars above him dipped down to meet it.

Under the bridge it was almost pitch dark. He stayed there for some time, hanging motionless on to a pile. Up to his neck in the cold water which still did not cool him down, he gradually managed to pierce the darkness and distinguish the strange forest of smooth trunks emerging from the surrounding eddies. It was no surprise; he was equally familiar with the view of the bridge from this angle.

'It's worth having a shot at it, sir, I'm sure. The best thing would be to float the charges down on a raft. It wouldn't be seen. We'd be in the water. Under the bridge there's nothing to worry about. The current's not strong enough to stop us swimming about between the piles. We could tie ourselves on, if necessary, to avoid being carried away. I went right across and measured the beams, sir. They're not very thick. Quite a small charge would do the trick—under the water. It's thick, muddy water, sir.'

'We'd have to place them fairly deep,' said Warden. 'The water might be clear on the day of the attack.'

He had done all the necessary groundwork. For over two hours he had sounded the piles, measuring them with a piece of string, calculating the gaps between them, making a note of the ones which would cause the most damage if destroyed, engraving in his mind every detail which might be of use in the plan of attack. On two occasions he had heard heavy steps above his head. A Japanese sentry was patrolling the platform. He had crouched against a pile and waited. The Jap had vaguely swept the river with an electric torch.

'Our only worry while we're approaching the target, sir, is if they light a lamp. But once we're under the bridge you can hear them coming a long way off. The sound of their footsteps is magnified by the water. That gives us plenty of time to make for one of the central piles.[1]

'Is the river deep?' asked Shears.

'Over six foot, sir. I dived to the bottom.'

'How would you set about it?'

'Here's my idea, sir. I don't think we can rely on an automatically detonated fog-signal. We couldn't camouflage the charges. The whole works will have to be under water. A goodish length of electric wire running along the river-bed and coming out on the bank—the right bank, sir, where it would be hidden by the undergrowth. I've found the ideal spot for that—a strip of virgin jungle where a man could easily lie up and wait. And there's a good view of the platform through a gap in the trees.'

'Why the right bank?' Shears broke in with a frown. 'That's the side where the camp is, unless I've got it all wrong. Why not the opposite bank, by the hill? It's covered in thick undergrowth, according to your report, and it would obviously be our line of withdrawal.'

'That's quite true, sir. But just have another look at the map. After this wide bend here the railway winds right round the hill after passing the bridge, and then comes downstream along the river. The jungle's been cleared between the line and the bank, and the ground's quite open. There's not enough cover in daylight. You'd have to lie up much further back, on the other side of the embankment at the foot of the hill. That would need too much wire, sir, and it couldn't be camouflaged where it crosses the line, at least not without a great deal of trouble.'

'I'm not too keen on the idea,' said Number One. 'Why not the left bank, but upstream from the bridge?'

'The bank's too high, sir, there's a steep cliff. And further up still there's that small native village. I went and had a look. I crossed the river again, and then the line. I made a slight detour to keep under cover and came back upstream from the bridge. It can't be done, sir. The only decent spot is on the right bank.'

'Good heavens!' exclaimed Warden. 'You must have spent the whole night wandering round the bridge.'

'Just about. But I was back in the jungle by first light and reached the O.P. early in the morning.'

'And what's your plan for the chap who has to lie up on

the right bank?' asked Shears. 'How does he manage to get away?'

'It wouldn't take a good swimmer more than three minutes to get across. That's how long it took me, sir; and the explosion would distract the Jap's attention. I think a rear party posted at the foot of the hill could cover his withdrawal. Once he's across the bit of open ground and on this side of the line, he's safe. A search party would never catch up with him in that jungle. I'm sure that's the best plan.'

Shears thought deeply for a long time as he studied Joyce's map.

'It's a plan worth considering,' he finally announced. 'Now that you've seen the spot for yourself, of course, you're in a position to tell us what you think of it. And the result will be worth taking a risk. What else did you see from your eyrie?'

III

The sun was well up by the time he had reached the top of the hill. His two guides, who had come back during the night, were anxiously waiting for him. He was worn out. He had lain down to rest for an hour, and had not woken up till the evening. He apologised when he mentioned this lapse on his part.

'Right. I suppose you slept again during the night? That was the best thing to do. And then you went back to the spot you had chosen next morning?'

'Yes, sir. I stayed on a day longer. There was still quite a lot I wanted to see.'

After devoting the first part of his reconnaissance to life-less objects he had felt an urge to look at living men. Until then he had been spellbound by the bridge and by the features in the landscape with which his future activity was now closely linked, but suddenly he had felt over-whelmed by the sight of his wretched comrades, whom he could see in the lens of his binoculars, reduced to an abject state of serfdom. He knew what Japanese methods were like in P.O.W. camps. There were stacks of secret reports describing the daily atrocities committed by the exultant enemy.

'Did you see anything unpleasant?' Shears asked him.

'No, sir; not that particular day. But I felt completely shattered at the thought that they had been working like this for months, in this climate, with not enough to eat, rotten huts to live in, no comfort at all, and the constant threat of—well, you can imagine what sort of punishment.'

He had observed each of the teams one after the other. He had scrutinised each individual through his glasses and had been horrified by the state they were in. Number One frowned as he said:

'In our job you can't afford to be too soft-hearted, Joyce.'

'I realise that, sir. But really, they're nothing but skin and bone. Most of them are covered in ulcers and jungle-sores. Some of them can hardly walk. No civilised person would even think of making men work in such a crippled state. You ought to see them, sir. It's enough to make you weep. The team pulling the rope to drive in the last few piles—absolute skeletons, sir. I've never seen such a ghastly sight. It's utterly criminal.'

'Don't worry,' said Shears, 'we'll soon get our own back.'

'Yet I couldn't help admiring them, sir. In spite of their obvious physical hardships, not one of them seemed really beaten. I had a good look at them. They make it a point of honour to behave as though their guards weren't there— that's exactly the impression I had. They behave as though the Japs just didn't exist. They're at work from dawn till dusk, and they've been at it like this for months, probably without a single day's rest. But they didn't look as though they'd lost hope. In spite of their ludicrous dress, in spite of their terrible physical condition, they couldn't be taken for slaves, sir. I could see the expression on their faces.'

All three fell silent for a moment, each lost in his own private thoughts.

'The British soldier's got any amount of guts when he's really up against it,' Warden finally observed.

'What else did you see?' said Shears.

'The officers, sir, the British officers. They're not being made to work. They're all in charge of their men, who seem to take more notice of them than of the Japanese guards. And they're all in full uniform.'

'In uniform!'

'Badges of rank and all, sir. I could count the pips on their shoulders.'

'Well, I'll be damned!' Shears exclaimed. 'The Siamese had told us about this bridge and I refused to believe them. In every other camp they're making all the prisoners work, irrespective of rank. Were there any senior officers?'

'A colonel, sir. That must be the Colonel Nicholson we've heard so much about, who was tortured when he first arrived. He was out there all day. I suppose he feels he should be on the spot in case there's any more trouble between his men and the Japs—because I bet you there has been trouble. I wish you could have seen those guards, sir. Monkeys dressed up as men! The way they drag their feet and slouch around, you'd never take them for anything human. Colonel Nicholson's a model of dignified behaviour. A born leader, that's how he struck me, sir.'

'He certainly must have an amazing influence, and exceptional qualities as well, to be able to keep the men's morale so high in such appalling conditions,' said Shears. 'I take my hat off to him.'

Surprise had followed surprise in the course of that day. Joyce went on with his story, obviously eager to let the others share in his astonishment and admiration.

'At one moment a prisoner from one of the groups furthest away came across the bridge to speak to the Colonel. When he was six paces off he snapped to attention, sir—in those funny clothes they all wear. Yet there was nothing funny about it. A Jap came rushing up, screaming and waving his rifle about in the air. I suppose that man must have left his team without permission. The Colonel just gave the guard one of those looks of his, sir. I saw the whole thing. The Jap thought better of it and shambled off. Incredible, isn't it? But that's not all. Just before dusk a Japanese colonel came on to the bridge—Saito, probably, the one who's said to be such a brute. Well, believe it or not, sir, when he went up to Colonel Nicholson, he almost kowtowed—there's no other word for it. There are certain ways you can tell . . . Colonel Nicholson saluted first, of course, but Saito smartly returned the salute—almost nervously, I could see! Then they walked up and down together. The Jap looked exactly like a junior officer being given his orders. It really cheered me up to see that, sir.'

'I can't say I'm sorry to hear about it myself,' Shears muttered.

'Here's to Colonel Nicholson,' Warden suddenly proposed, raising his glass.

'You're right, Warden, here's to him—and to the five or six hundred other poor beggars who are going through such hell because of this bloody bridge.'

'All the same, it's a pity they won't be able to help us.'

'It may be a pity, Warden, but you know what we're up against. We have to go through with it on our own. But let's get back to the bridge . . .'

They spent the whole evening discussing the bridge and studying Joyce's sketch-map in a fever of excitement, occasionally questioning him on some specific detail or other, which he promptly explained. He could have drawn every bit of the bridge and described every eddy in the river from memory. They then got down to the plan he had suggested, making a list of all the operations it would entail, working each of those out in detail, keeping a sharp look-out for any unforeseen snag that might conceivably crop up at the last moment. Then Warden went off to receive the incoming message on the W/T in the room next door. Joyce was silent for a moment.

'Look, sir,' he finally blurted out, 'I'm the best swimmer of the three, and now that I've been over the ground . . .'

'We'll discuss that later,' said Number One.

Shears realised that Joyce was at the end of his tether when he saw him stagger on his way to bed. After spending three days lying in the undergrowth, studying the lie of the land, he had set off on the return journey during the night and got back to camp by marching without stopping, except for a short halt for food. Even the Siamese had hardly been able to keep up with the pace he had set. They were now busy describing with admiration how the young white man had managed to walk them off their feet.

'You'd better get some rest,' said Number One. 'There's no point in working yourself to death before we start. We want to have you in proper shape when the time comes. Why did you return so quickly?'

'The bridge will probably be finished in less than a month from now.'

All of a sudden Joyce fell asleep, without even taking off the make-up which made him unrecognisable. Shears shrugged his shoulders and did not attempt to wake him. He sat there alone, working out the part that each of them would play in the scene shortly to be enacted in the Kwai valley. He had not yet come to any decision when Warden returned with a handful of messages which he had just deciphered.

'It looks as if the balloon will go up any day now, Shears. Information from H.Q.: the railway's almost finished along the whole of the line. The opening ceremony will probably be held in five or six weeks' time—a "first" train, crammed full of troops and V.I.P.s A nice little celebration. A fair amount of war material as well. Things are looking up. H.Q. have passed all your plans and are giving you a completely free hand. The R.A.F. won't interfere. We'll be getting a daily sitrep. The youngster's asleep, is he?'

'Yes, don't wake him up. He deserves a little rest. He did pretty well, you know. Tell me, Warden, do you think we can rely on him in *any* emergency?'

Warden thought the question over before answering.

'He looks all right to me. Of course, one can't be sure *beforehand*, you know that as well as I do. But I know what you're driving at. You want to know if he's capable of taking an important decision in a matter of seconds, or even less, and acting on it. But what made you bring that up?'

'Because he just said: "I'm the best swimmer of the three." And he's not shooting a line. It's true.'

'When I joined Force 316,' Warden growled, 'I didn't realise I would have to be a swimming champion in order to see some action. I'll put in a little practice on my next leave.'

'There's a psychological reason as well. If I don't give him his head, he'll lose confidence in himself, and then he'll be utterly useless. As you say, we can't be sure *beforehand* —even he can't be—and meanwhile he's dying to know. The main thing, of course, is whether he's got as much chance as we have of bringing it off. I think he has . . . and also a chance of getting away with it. We'll know for certain in a few days. I want to see what he looks like to-morrow. Let's not mention the bridge to him for the time being. I don't like the way he gets so worked up by the thought of those wretched prisoners. Oh, I know what you're going to say—what one feels has got nothing to do with how one behaves. All the same, he's rather inclined to get over-wrought, to let his imagination run riot, if you know what I mean. He broods a bit too much, that's his trouble.'

'You can't lay down a general rule for our sort of job,' Warden wisely observed. 'Sometimes you get good results by using a little imagination, and even by brooding. Not always, of course.'

IV

Colonel Nicholson also was worrying about the prisoners' state of health, and had come to the hospital to discuss the matter with the M.O.

'We can't go on like this, Clipton,' he said in a solemn,

almost threatening tone of voice. 'A man who's dangerously ill can't work, that's obvious; but all the same, there's a limit. You've now got half the personnel on the sick-list! How do you expect us to get the bridge finished in a month? It's well under way, I know, but there's still a lot of work to be done, and with the teams reduced to half-strength, we're just marking time. Even the ones who are still on the job don't seem up to the mark.'

'Look at them, sir,' said Clipton, who was so enraged by these words that he had to struggle to maintain his usual equanimity and show the necessary deference which the Colonel demanded of all his subordinates, no matter what their rank or position. 'If I had listened to the voice of my professional conscience, or simply to the voice of human decency, it wouldn't be half the personnel but the whole lot that I'd certify as unfit for work, especially this sort of work!'

For the first few months the bridge had gone forward at a spanking space, with only an occasional setback caused by Saito's moodiness. From time to time the Jap felt he ought to regain his position of authority and would try to give himself Dutch courage to overcome his complexes by a show of cruelty. But these outbursts had occurred less and less frequently since it was quite obvious that any attempt at violence did nothing but impede progress on the bridge. For a long time the work had been well ahead of the schedule laid down by Major Hughes and Captain Reeves, thanks to a collaboration which was efficient though not entirely free from friction. But the climate, the nature of the tasks imposed, the diet and the living conditions had all been a drain on the men's health.

Their physical condition was becoming a real anxiety. With no meat, apart from some decrepit old cow which the natives from the nearest village occasionally sold them, with no butter and no bread, the prisoners, whose meals sometimes consisted of rice and nothing else, had been gradually reduced to the skin-and-bone condition which Joyce had found so pitiful. The hard labour of heaving all day long on a rope to lift the heavy weight which dropped back again and again with an ear-splitting crash had become real torture to the men in that particular team. Some of the others were no better off, especially the ones who had to spend hours on end on a scaffolding, up to their waist in water, to hold the piles in position while the ram thudded down over and over again, deafening them each time.

Their morale was still fairly high, thanks to the fine example set by officers like Lieutenant Harper, who showed magnificent drive and energy, shouting cheerful words of encouragement all day long, and willingly lending a hand himself, although he was an officer, tugging at the rope with all his might so as to ease the burden of the weaker men. Their sense of humour was still in evidence on certain occasions, for instance whenever Captain Reeves appeared with his blue-print, foot-rule, spirit-level and other home-made instruments and crept along a rickety scaffolding just above water-level in order to take certain measurements, followed by the little Japanese engineer, who dogged his footsteps, copied every gesture he made, and solemnly recorded some figures in a note-book.

Since all the officers modelled themselves directly on the Colonel, the fate of the bridge was entirely in his capable hands. He knew this, and felt the justified pride of the leader who welcomes and seeks responsibility, but also takes on his own shoulders the burden of worries which that post of honour entails.

The growing sick-list was his chief anxiety. He saw his companies literally whittled down before his very eyes. Bit by bit, day by day, hour by hour, some of the living substance of each prisoner came apart from its individual organism to be swallowed up in the anonymous material universe. This universe of earth, monstrous vegetation, water and mosquito-infested swamp was not perceptibly affected by this human contribution. In arithmetical terms, it was a complete transfer of molecules, which was felt as a severe loss by each individual and could be measured in pounds' weight per man multiplied by five hundred, yet resulted in no appreciable total gain.

Clipton was frightened there might be a fatal epidemic such as cholera, which had broken out in some of the other camps. This scourge had so far been avoided, thanks to strict discipline, but there were still countless cases of malaria, dysentery and beri-beri. Every·day he was forced to declare a large number of men unfit for duty and to put them on the sick-list. In the hospital he managed to provide those who were able to eat with a fairly reasonable diet, thanks to a few Red Cross parcels which had escaped the prying hands of the Japanese and had been set aside for the patients. In any case a few days' off-duty was balm to some of the prisoners, who had worn themselves out on the ram and were consequently suffering from nervous prostration, seeing things and living in a continual nightmare.

Colonel Nicholson was fond of his men. At first he had backed Clipton up to the best of his ability so as to justify the size of the sick-list in the eyes of the Japanese. He had anticipated Saito's inevitable protests by demanding a greater effort from the men who were still fit.

But for some time now he had felt that Clipton was going too far. He openly suspected him of·abusing his medical privileges and of showing excessive leniency by certifying prisoners who could still be of some use as unfit for duty. The work was due to be completed in a month; this was no time for slacking off. He had come to the hospital that morning to inspect it personally, to thrash the matter out with Clipton and to put the M.O. on the right track—firmly, of course, but also with the courtesy which one had to show, after all, when approaching a staff officer on such a delicate issue.

'What about this chap, for instance?' he said, stopping to speak to one of the patients. 'What's wrong with you, my lad?'

He was walking between two rows of prisoners who lay on bamboo beds, either shivering with fever or in a state of coma, their cadaverous faces protruding from the threadbare blankets.

'Temperature of 104 last night, sir. Malaria.'

'Right, I see,' said the Colonel, moving on. 'And this man?'

'Jungle sores. I had to dig into his leg yesterday—with an ordinary knife; I haven't any other instruments. He's got a hole in him as large as a golf ball, sir.'

'So that was it,' muttered Colonel Nicholson. 'I thought I heard someone shrieking in the night.'

'That was it. Four of his pals had to hold him down. I hope I'll be able to save his leg, but it's touch and go,' he added, lowering his voice. 'Do you really want me to send him out to work, sir?'

'Don't talk rot, Clipton. Of course I don't. What you say, goes. But let's get this clear. I'm not trying to force sick and wounded men to work. But we must face this fact: we've got less than a month to finish the job we're doing. It'll require a superhuman effort, I know, but I can't help that. Consequently, each time you take one of the men off work, you make it harder for everyone else. You ought to bear that in mind every moment of the day, do you understand? Even if a man's not at the top of his form he can still make himself useful and help on light duties—the trimmings and finishing touches, for instance; the general wash and brush-up that Hughes will soon be organising, you know.'

'I suppose you're going to have the thing painted, sir?'

'Don't even think of such a thing, Clipton,' said the Colonel testily. 'The most we could do would be to give it a coating of lime—and a fine target that would make for the R.A.F., wouldn't it! You seem to forget **there's** a war on!'

'You're quite right sir, there's a war on.'

'No, there'll be nothing fancy about it. I'm all against that. All we want is a decent, properly finished job. That's what I came here to tell you, Clipton. You must make the men understand they've all got to pull their weight. This fellow now . . .'

'A nasty arm wound, sir, which he got from hoisting beams for that bridge of yours,' Clipton burst out. 'I've got twenty others like him on my hands. Naturally in their present state the wounds won't heal and they get infected. I've got nothing to treat them with . . .'

'I wonder,' persisted Colonel Nicholson, pursuing a single train of thought and overlooking Clipton's improper language, 'I wonder if in a case like this fresh air and light duties wouldn't do them more good than lying cooped up in this hut of yours. What do you think, Clipton? After all it's not our usual policy to send a man to hospital just because he's scratched his arm. If you stop to think for a moment, Clipton, I'm sure you'll feel the same as I do.'

'Not our policy, sir! No, not our policy!'

He raised his arms in a gesture of impotent despair. The Colonel took him aside, away from the patients, into the ante-room which served as a surgery, and went on pleading his case, using every argument available to a commander who wants to persuade rather than give orders. Finally, since Clipton seemed far from convinced, he put forward his most cogent reason: if Clipton insisted on pursuing this course, the Japanese would take it on themselves to evacuate the hospital completely and would show no discrimination in the process.

'Saito has threatened to take drastic steps,' he explained.

That was a white lie. Having at last realised that violence had no result, Saito had now stopped using it and, in his heart of hearts, was delighted to see the best installation on the whole line being built under his direction. Colonel Nicholson had indulged in this distortion of the truth, even though it pricked his conscience. He could not afford to disregard a single factor which might accelerate the completion of the bridge—this bridge representing the dauntless sort of spirit which never acknowledges defeat but always has some inner resource to draw on as proof of its invincibility, this bridge which needed only a few more yards before it would straddle the Kwai valley in a single unbroken line.

Faced with this threat, Clipton cursed the Colonel but was forced to yield. He discharged about a quarter of the patients, in spite of the terrible moral problem that confronted him each time he had to make a choice. In this way he sent back to work a crowd of limping cripples, walking wounded and malaria cases still shaking with fever but capable of dragging themselves along.

They did not complain. The Colonel had the sort of faith which moves mountains, builds pyramids, cathedrals or even bridges, and makes dying men go to work with a smile on their lips. They succumbed to his appeal that they should pull their weight. They went down to the river without a murmur. Some of the poor devils, with one arm out of action thanks to a dirty or slipshod dressing, seized the rope of the ram with their only good hand and tugged at it all together with what remained of their will and strength, putting all their reduced weight behind it, contributing the additional sacrifice on this painful effort to the sum total of suffering which was slowly bringing the River Kwai bridge to a successful conclusion.

With this fresh impetus the bridge was soon finished. All that remained now was what the Colonel called the 'trimmings,' which would give the construction that 'finished' look in which the practised eye can at once recognise, in no matter what part of the world, the craftsmanship of the European and the Anglo-Saxon sense of perfection.

PART FOUR

I

A few weeks after Joyce's expedition Warden followed the same route as the lieutenant and, like him, reached the O.P. after an exhausting climb. It was his turn now to lie flat on his face in the ferns and observe the Kwai bridge down below.

Warden was anything but romantic. At first he gave no more than a rapid glance, just sufficient to enable him to recognise with satisfaction the construction that Joyce had depicted and to confirm that it was now complete. There were four partisans with him. He told them he did not need them for the moment. They sat down in their favourite position, lit their water-pipes and watched him quietly get down to work.

He first set up his W/T aerial and tuned in to several stations. One of these, an absolute boon in occupied territory, gave him a daily intelligence report on the forthcoming departure of the big convoy which was to inaugurate the Burma-Siam railway. The messages he received were encouraging : the orders still stood.

After that he arranged his sleeping-bag and mosquito-net as comfortably as possibly, carefully laid out the contents of his sponge-bag, then did the same for Shears who was to join him on this hill-top. Warden was a man of foresight. older than Joyce and more level-headed. He was also more experienced. He knew the jungle from the various expeditions he had been on during his pre-war vacations. He knew how highly a white man values his tooth-brush at certain times and how much longer he can carry on if properly installed and if fortified by a cup of tea in the morning. If they were hard pressed after the attack, they would have to jettison these goods and chattels of the civilised world; they would no longer be needed. But they would have helped to keep them fighting fit up to the moment they went into action. Satisfied with his arrangements, he ate some food, slept for three hours, then went back to the O.P. and tried to think of the best method of carrying out his mission.

In accordance with Joyce's plan, which, after countless modifications, had been finally adopted by all three of them and on which Number One had now decided to take action, the Force 316 team had split up. Shears, Joyce and two Siamese volunteers, accompanied by a few porters, had set off in single file for a point on the river upstream from the bridge, so as to avoid launching the explosives in the vicinity of the camp. They had gone rather far out of their way, making a wide detour to by-pass some native settlements. The four men were to move down to the bridge at night in order to prepare the material. (It would be a gross mistake to think that blowing up a bridge is a simple operation.) Joyce was to remain in hiding on the enemy bank and there wait for the train. Shears was to rejoin Warden and, with him, share the responsibility of covering the withdrawal.

Warden was to remain at the O.P., maintain radio contact, observe what went on round the bridge and reconnoitre possible positions from which to give Joyce covering fire. The scope of his mission was not strictly limited. Number One had allowed him a certain amount of initiative. He would have to act for the best according to the circumstances.

'If you see any chance of following up with a subsidiary attack,' Shears had told him, 'then I won't try to stop you —provided, of course, that there's no risk of your being discovered. The principles of Force 316 still hold good. But the bridge is our number one target and on no account must you jeopardise our chances of success in that direction. I'm relying on you to be sensible and at the same time forceful.'

He knew he could rely on Warden to be both sensible and forceful. Whenever there was time, Warden methodically weighed up the consequences of every gesture he made.

After an initial reconnaissance of the sky-line Warden decided to place his pocket artillery—two light mortars—right on top of the hill and to man this post during the attack with the two Siamese partisans, so that the wreckage of the train, the troops trying to escape after the explosion, and the soldiers rushing up to help them, would all be under constant fire.

This was perfectly in keeping with the implicit instructions contained in Number One's reference to the principles of Force 316. These principles could be summed up as follows: 'Never assume an operation is complete in itself; never be satisfied while there's still a chance, however slight, of causing the enemy further alarm and despondency.' (The typically Anglo-Saxon 'finishing touches' were as much in evidence in this sphere of activity as elsewhere.) Now, in this case it was obvious that a tail of mortar shells falling on the survivors, like bolts from the blue, would be calculated to demoralise the enemy completely. The O.P., which commanded the whole valley, was almost miraculously placed from this point of view. At the same time Warden saw yet another advantage in prolonging the attack: it would divert the enemy's attention and so indirectly help to cover Joyce's withdrawal.

Warden spent a long time creeping through the ferns and wild rhododendrons before finding gun-emplacements entirely to his satisfaction. When he did find them, he called up the Siamese, chose two of them, and told them exactly what they would have to do when the time came. They were quick in the uptake and seemed to like the idea.

It was about four in the afternoon by the time Warden completed his preparations. He then started to think about the subsequent arrangements to be made, when he heard the sound of music in the valley. He returned to his observation, his field-glasses trained on foe and friend alike. The bridge was deserted, but there was something strange going on in the camp, over on the far side of the river. Warden at once realised that, in order to celebrate the successful conclusion of their labours, the prisoners had been allowed, or perhaps even obliged, to throw a party. A signal received a few days ago had notified him of these festivities decreed by the loving kindness of His Imperial Majesty.

The music emanated from some instrument which must have been knocked together by a local craftsman, but the hand plucking the strings belonged to a European. Warden knew the barbaric tunes of the Japanese well enough not to be mistaken. Besides, the sound of singing soon reached his ears. In feeble, faltering tones, but with an unmistakable accent, a voice was singing an old Scottish ballad. The words echoed round the valley and were taken up in chorus. This pathetic concert heard in the solitude of his O.P. moved Warden to the point of tears. He made a conscious effort to repel these gloomy thoughts and managed to drive them out of his mind by concentrating instead on the requirements of his mission. He lost all interest in what was happening inside the camp, except in so far as it effected the impending attack.

Shortly before sundown it looked as if a banquet was being prepared. Prisoners began to crowd round the cookhouse. There was a noticeable stir in the direction of the Japanese quarters as well, where several soldiers were rushing about, shouting and laughing. The Japanese, it appeared, were also preparing to celebrate the conclusion of their labours.

Warden's mind worked fast. His cool, calculating temperament did not prevent him from pouncing on the first opportunity that occurred. He made the necessary arrangements for going into action that very night, having suddenly decided to follow a plan which he had thought of long before he reached the O.P. His profound understanding of human nature told him that in a God-forsaken patch of jungle like this, with a chronic alcoholic like Saito in command, and with soldiers subject to a régime almost as ruthless as that of the prisoners themselves, every Jap in the place was bound to be blind drunk by midnight. Here was an exceptionally favourable opportunity for him to take individual action, with a minimum of risk in accordance with Number One's instructions, and to lay a few of those subsidiary traps, which give to the main attack that additional zest to which every member of Force 316 is partial. Warden weighed up the pros and cons, came to the conclusion that it would be criminal not to exploit this miraculous coincidence, decided to move down to the river, and started making up a small charge . . . for, even against his better judgment, why should not he too, just for once, have a close view of that bridge?

He reached the foot of the hill shortly before midnight. The party had ended exactly as he expected it would. He had been able to follow each stage of it from the increasing din punctuating his own silent progress: savage yells, like a parody of the English singing, had stopped some time ago. The silence was now complete. He called a final halt and listened carefully, crouching with two partisans who had accompanied him behind the last curtain of trees not far from the railway line, which at this point ran along the river after crossing the bridge, just as Joyce had described it. Warden signalled to the Siamese. Carrying the sabotage material, the three men cautiously moved off in the direction of the railway.

Warden was convinced he could perform the operation in complete security. There was no sign of the enemy on this bank. The Japanese had enjoyed such complete peace in this out-of-the-way corner that they had lost all sense of danger. By now all the soldiers, and all the officers too, must have passed out, all of them blind drunk. But just to make sure, Warden posted one of the Siamese as a sentry, then methodically got down to work, assisted by the other.

What he had in mind was a straightforward, text-book operation. It was the first lesson taught in the Plastic and Destructions Company's special school in Calcutta. It is quite a simple job to loosen the gravel which is used as ballast on a railway line from either side of the rails and from underneath them, so as to make a small cavity capable of holding a plastic charge fastened to the inside of the metals. The properties of this chemical compound are such that a two-pound charge, if cleverly placed, is all that is needed. The energy stored in that small amount is rapidly released, by the action of a detonator, in the form of a gas which reaches a speed of several thousand feet per second. The strongest steel is incapable of standing up to the splintering effect of this sudden expansion.

The detonator, then, is inserted in the plastic. (Pressing it in is as easy as sliding a knife through a pat of butter.) A length of so-called 'instantaneous' fuse connects it to a wonderfully simple little mechanism which is likewise hidden in a hole made underneath the rail. This device consists of two blades kept apart by a strong spring, with a primer inserted between them. One of the blades is placed against the metal, while the other is firmly wedged with a stone. The detonating cord itself is buried below the surface. A team of two experts can lay this charge in less than half an hour. If the work is done carefully, the trap is invisible.

When one of the wheels of the engine presses down on the mechanism, the two blades are crushed together. The primer then sets the detonator off through the action of the instantaneous cord. The plastic explodes. A length of steel is reduced to powder. The train is derailed. With a little luck and with a slightly larger charge, the engine can be overturned. One of the advantages of this method is that the mechanism is released by the train itself, thus enabling the agent who has laid it to be a mile or more away at the time. Another is that it cannot go off prematurely if an animal treads on it. A really heavy weight, like a locomotive or a railway-coach, is needed.

Warden, in his logical systematic way, pursued the following argument: the first train will come from Bangkok along the right bank and so, in theory, will be blown up at the same time as the bridge and crash into the river. So much for target number one. The line is consequently cut, and traffic comes to a standstill. The Japanese then work like fiends to repair the damage. They are anxious to repair it as quickly as possible in order to open up the line

again and avenge this outrage, which is also a serious blow
to their prestige. They rush forward any amount of labour-
gangs and work without stopping. They toil away for days,
for weeks, perhaps even for months. When the line is at
last cleared, and the bridge rebuilt, another convoy comes
along. This time the bridge holds together. But a little later
—the next train to cross blows up. That is bound to cause
an adverse psychological effect, apart from material damage. Warden lays a slightly larger charge than is strictly
necessary, and places it so that the train will come off the
rails close to the river bank. If all goes well, the engine and
some of the coaches will land in the water.

Warden quickly completed these initial stages of his
work. He was a past-master at this sort of job, having
trained himself to shift the gravel without making a sound
before moulding the plastic and setting the booby-trap. He
operated almost mechanically and was pleased to find that
the Siamese partisan, though new to the game, was never-
the less an able assistant. His instruction had been good—
much to the delight of Professor Warden. There was still
some time to go before first light. He had brought with him
a second contraption of the same type but slightly different,
which he placed a few hundred yards further up the line in
the opposite direction to the bridge. It would be criminal
not to take full advantage of a night like this.

Warden had shown his usual foresight. After two attacks
in the same sector the enemy usually got suspicious and
proceeded to inspect the line systematically. But one never
knew. Sometimes, on the contrary, he could not imagine
the possibility of a third outrage, precisely because there
had already been two. In any case, if the trap was well
camouflaged, it might escape the most searching scrutiny—
unless the search-party reluctantly decide to rake through
every bit of gravel in the ballast. Warden set his second
'toy,' which differed from the first in that it was fitted with
a device to vary the effects of the explosion and cause another sort of alarm. The mechanism worked on a kind of
delayed-action principle. The first train did not set it off, but
simply started the mechanism working. The detonator and

plastic themselves were only affected by the weight of the following train. It was quite clear what the Force 316 technicians had in mind when they perfected this ingenious device which so delighted Warden's rational mentality. Quite often, when a line had been repaired after a whole series of accidents, the enemy sent the next important convoy through behind a screen of a couple of coaches loaded with stones and pulled by a useless old engine. Nothing untoward happened to the leading train. And so the enemy was convinced that his run of bad luck was over. Full of confidence, and without any further security measure, he launched the train that really mattered and hey-presto, the train that really mattered blew up!

'Never assume an operation is complete unless the enemy has been caused as much alarm and despondency as possible' was the *leitmotiv* of the Plastic and Destructions Company, Ltd. 'Always strive to multiply the number of unpleasant surprises and to invent fresh traps so as to sow confusion among the enemy just when he thinks he has at last been left in peace' was the firm's ceaseless exhortation. Warden had taken these doctrines to heart. After setting his second trap and leaving no trace of it, he again wracked his brains and tried to think of yet another trick to play.

He had brought with him a few other 'toys,' just in case. He had several specimens of one of these, consisting of a round of ammunition fitted into a loose board which pivoted on its axis and snapped back on to a second, fixed, board pierced with a nail. These were anti-personnel devices. They were hidden under a thin layer of earth. They were the most simple sort of mechanism imaginable. The weight of one man was all that was needed to snap the round down on to the firing-pin. The bullet went off and pierced the man's foot or, with any luck, hit him in the forehead if he happened to be walking leaning forward. The instructors in the special school in Calcutta recommended scattering large numbers of these 'toys' in the neighbourhood of a 'prepared' railway line. After the explosion, when the survivors (there were bound to be a few) were rushing about in panic, the traps would go off and add to their confusion.

Warden would have liked to get rid of the whole lot as cunningly as possible, but his caution and reason prompted him to abandon this final delight. There was a risk of their being discovered, and the priority target was too important to warrant such a risk. A sentry coming across one of these traps would be enough to put the Japs on their guard against a possible sabotage attack.

Dawn was approaching. Warden wisely but reluctantly decided to go no further and started back for the O.P. He was fairly pleased to be leaving behind him a well-prepared area seasoned with spices designed to give an added zest to the main attack.

II

One of the partisans made a sudden movement. He had heard an unusual crackling in the forest of giant ferns which covered the hill-top. For a few seconds the four Siamese kept absolutely still. Warden had seized his tommy-gun and stood ready for any eventuality. Three low whistles were heard a little below them. One of the Siamese whistled back, then waved his arm and turned to Warden.

'Number One,' he said.

Presently Shears and a couple of natives joined the group at the O.P.

'What's the latest?' he anxiously asked as soon as he caught sight of Warden.

'Everything under control. Nothing new. I've been here three days. It's all set for to-morrow. The train leaves Bangkok some time during the night and should get here about ten in the morning. What about you?'

'Everything's ready,' said Shears, lowering himself to the ground with a sigh of relief.

He had been horribly afraid that the Japanese plans might have been changed at the last moment. Warden too had been on tenterhooks since the evening before. He knew that the bridge was being prepared that night and had spent hours listening blindly for the slightest sound from the River Kwai, thinking of his two friends at work in the water just below him, constantly weighing up their chances of success, visualising each successive stage of the operation, and trying to think of any snag that might possibly crop up. He had heard nothing unusual. According to the programme, Shears was to rejoin him at first light. It was now past ten o'clock.

'I'm glad you've turned up at last. I was getting a little worried.'

'We were hard at it all night.'

Warden looked at him more closely and saw that he was utterly exhausted. His clothes, which were still damp, steamed in the sun. His drawn features, the dark circles under his eyes, the growth of beard on his chin, made him look like nothing on earth. He handed him a flask of brandy and noticed how he fumbled as he seized it. His hands were covered with scratches and cuts, the dead-white skin wrinkled and hanging in strips. He could hardly move his fingers. Warden gave him a dry shirt and a pair of shorts which he had put out for him, then waited.

'You're quite sure nothing's planned for to-day?' Shears repeated.

'Absolutely. Another signal came in this morning.'

Shears took a gulp, then gingerly started massaging his limbs.

'Rather a tough job,' he remarked with a shudder. I think I'll remember that cold water for the rest of my life. But everything went off all right.'

'What about the youngster?'

'The youngster was terrific. Didn't let up for a second. He was at it harder than I was, yet showed no sign of fatigue. He's now in position on the right bank. He insisted on settling in at once and staying put until the train arrives.'

'Supposing they get wind of him?'

'He's well concealed. It's a risk, I know, but it's worth

it. We've got to avoid a lot of movement round the bridge at this stage. And then the train might turn up earlier than we think. I'm sure they won't catch him napping to-day. He's young, and he's tough. He's lying up in a thicket which can only be reached from the river, and the bank there is steep. We can probably see the place from here. All he can see, through a gap in the branches, is the bridge. But he'll be able to hear the train approaching.'

'Did you go there yourself?'

'I went with him. He was right. It's a perfect position.'

Shears took out his field-glasses and tried to spot the place in a landscape which was strange to him.

'It's hard to pin-point it,' he said. 'It all looks so different from here. But I think it's over there, about ten yards behind that large red tree with its branches trailing in the water.'

'So now everything depends on him.'

'Yes, everything depends on him, and I feel completely confident.'

'Has he got his knife?'

'He's got his knife. And I'm sure he'll be capable of using it.'

'One can never really tell till the time comes.'

'I know one can't. All the same, I'm pretty sure.'

'And afterwards?'

'It took me five minutes to get across the river, but he swims nearly twice as fast as I do. We'll be able to cover his withdrawal.'

Warden told Shears what arrangements he had made. The evening before, he had climbed down from the O.P., this time before it was quite dark, but had not gone as far as the stretch of flat, open ground. On his way he had selected a suitable spot for the team's light machine-gun and had reconnoitred positions for the partisans who were to provide rifle fire in the event of a counter-attack. Each position had been carefully noted down. This barrage, in conjunction with the mortar shells, would provide ample protection for quite a long time.

Number One approved of the plan in general. Then,

since he felt too tired to sleep, he described to his friend how the previous night's operation had been carried out. As he listened carefully to this account, Warden felt almost relieved that he himself had not taken part in the preparations. Meanwhile, there was nothing else for them to do until the next day. As they had said, everything now depended on Joyce—on Joyce and the fortunes of war. They tried hard to curb their impatience and to stop worrying about the principal actor, who now lay hidden in the bushes over on the enemy bank.

As soon as he had decided to put his plan into action, Number One had drawn up a detailed programme. He had assigned the various roles so as to enable each individual member of the team to think out in advance what he would have to do and to rehearse each move that he would have to make. In this way, when the time came, they would all be able to keep their minds free to deal with any unforeseen eventuality.

It would be childish to think that a bridge can be blown up without a great many preparations. Working from Joyce's sketch and notes, Warden, like Captain Reeves, had made a plan—a destruction plan : a large-scale drawing of the bridge in which every pile was numbered and every charge marked in at the exact spot where it would be needed, the intricate network of electric wire and detonating cord which would set the whole thing off being indicated in red pencil. Each of them soon had this plan engraved on his memory.

But these paper-work preparations had not been sufficient for Number One. He had made them go through several rehearsals at night from an old derelict bridge lying across a stream not far from their camp, the charges, of course, being represented by sacks of earth. The men who were to fix the explosives in position—himself, Joyce and two local volunteers—had practised swimming silently, pushing in front of them a light bamboo raft specially built for the purpose on which all the kit was fastened. Warden was the umpire. He had been quite ruthless and had made them repeat the drill until the operation was a hundred per cent perfect. The four men had got used to working in the water without making a splash, fastening the dummy charges firmly on to the piles and connecting them together by means of the intricate network of fuses worked out in the destruction plan. At last they had managed to do it to Number One's satisfaction. All that now remained was to prepare the genuine material and see to a mass of important details, such as waterproof sheeting for whatever needed protecting from the damp.

The party had then started off. Along paths known only to themselves, the guides had taken them to a point on the river a long way upstream from the bridge, where the launching could take place in complete security. Several native volunteers were acting as porters.

The plastic was made up into twelve-pound charges, each of which had to be fastened to a separate pile. The destruction plan catered for the preparation of six consecutive piles in each row, making a total of twenty-four charges. All the supporting beams would thus be shattered for a stretch of nearly thirty yards, which would be quite sufficient to bring the bridge down under the weight of a train. Shears had wisely brought a dozen extra charges in case of accident. They might eventually be fixed in some suitable position to cause the enemy further alarm. He was not one to forget the maxims of Force 316.

These various quantities had not been chosen at random. They had been determined after much calculation and long discussion, and were based on the measurements that Joyce had taken during his reconnaissance. A formula, which all three knew by heart, gave the weight of charge required for shattering a beam of any given material, according to its shape and size. In this case six pounds of plastic would have been enough, in theory. With eight, the margin of security would have been ample for any ordinary operation. Number One eventually decided to increase the amount still further.

He had good reasons for adopting such measures. Another of the Plastic and Destructions Company's principles was to add a little on to every figure provided by the technicians. At the end of the theoretical training Colonel Green, who ran the Calcutta school at a very high level, used to deliver a short address on this subject, based on common sense and his personal experience of engineering.

'When you work out the weight needed by means of the formula,' he would say, 'make a generous allowance—then add even a little more on. On a tricky operation you make absolutely certain. If you're in the least doubtful it's better to use a hundred pounds too much than a pound too little. You'd look pretty silly if, after slaving away, for several nights perhaps, in order to prepare the target, after risking your life and your men's lives, after getting so far after God knows how many difficulties—you'd look pretty silly if, for the sake of saving a few pounds of explosive, the destruction was only a partial success—beams knocked about a bit but still in position, and so quite easy to repair. I'm speaking from personal experience. That's what happened to me once, and I can't think of anything in the world that's more demoralising.'

Shears had sworn he would never allow such a disaster to happen to him, and he generously applied the principle. On the other hand one had to guard against going to the opposite extreme and cluttering oneself up with a lot of useless material when there was only a small team available.

In theory, the launching of the material presented no difficulty. One of the many qualities of plastic is that it has about the same density as water. A swimmer can easily tow quite a large amount of it behind him.

They had reached the River Kwai at dawn. The porters had been sent back. The four men had waited till nightfall, hidden in the undergrowth.

'The hours must have dragged by,' said Warden. 'Did you manage to get to sleep?'

'Hardly at all. We tried to, but you know what's it like just before zero hour. Joyce and I spent the whole afternoon chatting. I wanted to keep his mind off the bridge. We had the whole night to think about that.'

'What did you talk about?' said Warden, who wanted to know every detail.

'He told me a little about his civilian life. A rather sad type at heart, that lad. A pretty dull career on the whole—draughtsman in a big engineering firm; nothing brilliant about it, and he doesn't pretend there was. A sort of glorified office-boy. I'd always imagined it was something like that. Two dozen chaps of the same age sitting all day long over their drawing-boards in a communal work-room—can't you see what it was like? When he wasn't drawing, he was working out sums—with formulae and a slide-rule. Nothing particularly exciting. I don't think he was too keen on the job—he seems to have welcomed the war as the chance of his lifetime. Strange that a chap chained to a desk should have landed up in Force 316.'

'Well, after all, there are professors in it as well,' said Warden. 'I've known quite a few like him. They're not necessarily the worst of the bunch.'

'And not necessarily the best either. You can't make a general rule about it. But he's not at all bitter when he talks about his past. Just rather sad, that's all.'

'He's all right, I'm sure. What sort of drawing did he have to do?'

'By a strange coincidence the firm had something to do with bridges. Not wooden bridges, of course. And they didn't handle construction work either. Articulated bridges in metal—a standard model. They used to make them in separate pieces and deliver them all together to the contractors—just like a meccano set! He was never out of the office. For two years before the war he drew the same piece over and over again. Specialisation and all the rest of it—you can imagine what it was like. He didn't find it terribly exciting. It wasn't even a very big piece—a girder, that's what he said. His job was to work out the shape that would give the greatest resistance for the smallest weight of metal, at least that's what I understood him to say. I don't know anything about the subject. It was a question of economy—the firm didn't like wasting material. He spent two years doing that—a boy of his age! You should have heard him talk about that girder! His voice was trembling. You know, Warden, I think the girder was partly responsible for his enthusiasm for the present job.'

'I must admit,' said Warden, 'I've never seen anyone quite so keen on the idea of destroying a bridge. I'm beginning to think, Shears, that Force 316 is a heaven-sent opportunity for men like that. If it didn't exist, we'd have had to invent it. Take yourself, now; if you hadn't been fed up with regimental soldiering . . .'

'And if you, for instance, had been completely satisfied with lecturing at a university . . . Well, whatever the reason, at the outbreak of the war he was still completely absorbed in that girder. He told me quite seriously that in two years he had succeeded in saving a pound and a half of metal, on paper. That wasn't too bad, it seems, but the firm thought he could do still better. He would have had to go on like that for months on end. He joined up during the first few days. When he heard about Force 316, he could hardly wait. And people still say there's no truth in vocation! It's a funny thing, though. If it hadn't been for that girder, he probably wouldn't at this very moment be lying flat on his face in the undergrowth a hundred yards from the enemy, with a knife in his belt and an instrument of wholesale destruction by his side.'

III

Shears and Joyce had chatted like this all day, while the two Siamese conversed in an undertone about the expedition. Shears had an occasional twinge of conscience, wondering whether he had chosen the right man for the most important role, the one who of the three of them had the best chance of succeeding; or whether he had simply succumbed to the earnestness of his entreaties.

'Are you quite sure you'll be able to act as decisively as Warden or myself no matter what the circumstance?' he had solemnly asked for the last time.

'I'm absolutely certain now, sir. You must give me this chance.'

Shears had not pressed the point and had not reconsidered his decision.

They had started the launching just before dusk. The bank was deserted. The bamboo raft—which they had themselves built, since they trusted no one else to do the job properly—consisted of two separate, parallel sections, to make it more easy to carry through the jungle. They slid it into the river and fastened the two halves together by lashing a couple of shafts across them. When in position, they made a rigid platform. Then they fixed the charges on as firmly as possible. There were other parcels containing the rolls of cord, the battery, electric wire and the generator. The fragile material, of course, was wrapped in waterproof sheeting. As for the detonators, Shears had brought an extra set. He had given one to Joyce and carried the other himself. They were wearing them in their belts. These were the only really tricky things to carry, plastic being in principle immune to rough handling.

'All the same, you must have felt uncomfortably weighed down with those parcels round your waist,' Warden observed.

'You know, one never thinks of that sort of thing—anyway that was the least dangerous part of the voyage. Yet we were shaken about, I can tell you. Damn those Siamese who promised us an easy stretch of water!'

According to the information of the natives, they had calculated that the trip would last less than half an hour. So they had not set out until it was pitch dark. Actually, they had taken over an hour, and it was heavy going all the way. The current in the River Kwai, except for a calm stretch round the bridge, was like a torrent. As soon as they started, the rapids swept them away into the darkness, past rocks which they could not avoid, while they clung desperately on to their precious, dangerous cargo.

'If I had known what the river was like, I should have chosen a different line of approach and taken the risk of launching the stuff nearer the bridge. It's always the simple information like this that turns out false, Warden, whether it comes from the native sources or European. I've often noticed that. I was led up the garden path once again. You can't imagine how hard it was to manoeuvre the submarine in that torrent.'

The 'submarine' was the name they had given the raft, which, weighted down at each end with bits of iron, floated half under water most of the time. Its trim had been carefully worked out so as to make it only just buoyant when launched. In this way the mere pressure of a finger was enough to submerge it completely.

'In the first rapids, which sounded as loud as Niagara, we were tossed around, buffeted about and whirled over and under the submarine from one bank to the other, sometimes scraping the river-bed, at other times the branches. When I got things more or less under control (which took me some time—I was half-drowned) I ordered each man to hang on to the submarine and not let go at any price, to concentrate on that and nothing else. That was all we could do, and it's a miracle no one had his head bashed in. A really splendid tonic, just what we needed to put us in the right mood for the serious job ahead. The waves were like a storm in mid-ocean. I was nearly sea-sick; and there was no way we could avoid the obstacles. Sometimes—would you believe it, Warden—sometimes we could not even tell if we were going backwards or forwards. Do you think that's strange? When the river begins to narrow and the jungle closes over you, I defy you to know for certain what direction you're moving in. We were being swept down with the current, you'll say. Yes, but compared to us, the water, apart from the waves, was as calm as a lake. It was only the obstacles that gave up some idea of our direction and speed—when we bumped into them. A question of relativity! I wonder if you can imagine . . .'

It must have been an extraordinary sensation. He did his best to describe it as accurately as possible. Warden was intrigued as he listened to him.

'I can well imagine it, Shears. And the raft held together?'

'Another miracle! I could hear it cracking whenever my

head happened to be above water-level, but it did hold together—except for a second. It was the youngster who
saved the situation. He's first class, Warden. It was like this.
At the end of the first rapids, when we were just beginning to get used to the dark, we crashed into a huge rock
bang in the middle of the river. We were literally thrown
up in the air, Warden, on a cushion of water, before being
snatched down again by the current and dragged over to
one side. I should never have thought it possible. I saw the
obstruction looming up when we were only a few feet off.
There was no time. All I could think of doing was shooting
out my legs and straddling a bit of bamboo. The two Siamese were chucked off. Fortunately we picked them up again
a little further down. Pure luck! But do you know what he
did? He only had a split second to think. He flung himself
flat on his stomach right across the raft. Do you know
why, Warden? To keep the two halves together. Yes, one
of the ropes had snapped. The shafts were slipping and
the two bits were beginning to come apart. The bump must
have shaken them loose. A disaster—he took it all in at a
glance. He thought fast. He had the sense to act and the
guts to hold on. He was in front of me. I saw the submarine
rise out of the water and leap into the air, like a salmon
making upstream—just like that; with him underneath,
clinging on to the bamboo sticks. He did not let go. Later
on we fixed the bits together as best we could. In that
position, you realise, his detonators were in direct contact
with the plastic, and he must have taken a hell of a toss. I
saw him right above my head, I tell you. Like a flash of
lightning! That was the only moment I was conscious of
the explosives we were carrying. It didn't matter, of course.
There wasn't the slightest danger, I'm sure. But he had
realised that in a split second. He's an exceptional chap,
Warden, I know it. He's bound to succeed.'

'A wonderful combination of sound judgment and quick
reflex-action,' Warden agreed.

Shears went on in a low voice:

'He's bound to succeed, Warden. This job is part of him,
and no one can stop him going through with it. It's his own

personal show. He knows that. You and I are only on-
lookers now. We've had our day. All we've got to think
about now is making his task as easy as possible. The fate
of the bridge is in good hands.'

At the end of the first rapids there had been a lull, during
which they had put the raft together again. Then they had
another rough passage through a narrow gap in the river.
They had wasted some time in front of a pile of rocks
which obstructed the proper flow of water, causing a vast
slow-moving whirlpool upstream, in which they had been
caught for several minutes without being able to move any
further.

At last they had escaped from this trap. The river had
widened, going suddenly sluggish, which had given them
the impression of being washed out on to a huge, calm lake.
Soon afterwards they had caught sight of the bridge.

Shears broke off and gazed in silence at the valley.

'Strange to be looking at it like this, from above, and
seeing the whole thing. It's got quite a different appearance
when you're down there at night. All I saw of it were
separate bits flashing past, one after the other. It's those bits
that matter to us right now—and also afterwards, for that
matter. But when we arrived it was outlined against the sky
surprisingly clearly. I was scared stiff someone would see
us. I felt we were as visible as though it was broad daylight.
Just an illusion, of course. We were up to our necks in the
water. The submarine was submerged. It even showed
signs of sinking completely. Some of the bamboos had
caved in. But everything went off all right. There was no
light. We glided silently into the shadow of the bridge.
Not even a bump. We tied the raft up to one of the central
piles and got down to work. We were already quite numb
with cold.'

'Any particular trouble?' asked Warden.

'No *particular* trouble. I suppose, Warden—unless you
think this sort of job is all in a day's work.'

He fell silent again, as though hypnotised by the bridge,
which he could see still shining in the sun, the light-

coloured wood showing clear above the yellowish water.

'All this seems to be happening in a dream, Warden I've had that feeling before. When the time comes, you wonder if it's true, if it's real, if the charges are really there, if it's really true that one touch to the plunger of the generator is all that's needed. It all seems so utterly impossible. There's Joyce, less than a hundred yards away from the enemy lines. There he is, behind that tree, watching the bridge. I bet he hasn't moved an inch since I left. Just think what could happen before to-morrow, Warden. If a Jap soldier should happen to amuse himself by chasing a snake into the jungle . . . I shouldn't have left him there. He shouldn't have got into position until this evening.'

'He's got his knife,' said Warden. 'It's up to him. Tell me about the rest of that night.'

After a long immersion in water a man's skin becomes so soft that mere contact with a rough object is enough to bruise it. Hands are particularly sensitive. The slightest scrape tears strips off the fingers. The first difficulty had been untying the ropes which had been used to fasten the kit on to the raft. They were rough native cords bristling with thorny prickles.

'It sounds like child's play, Warden, but in the state we were in . . . And when you've got to work under water, and without making a noise. Look at my hands. Joyce's are the same.'

Once again he peered out over the valley. He could not stop thinking about the other man waiting over there on the enemy bank. He lifted his hands, examined the deep cuts which had congealed in the sun, then, with a shrug of his shoulders, went on with his account.

They had both carried sharp knives, but their frozen fingers could hardly handle them. And then, even though plastic is a 'tame' explosive, digging into it with a metal instrument is not exactly recommended. Shears had soon realised that the two Siamese were not going to be of any further use.

'I was frightened of that all along, and had said so to the

youngster before we set off. I told him we would have to rely on ourselves and no one else to get the job done. They were completely done for. They stood there shivering and clinging to one of the piles. I sent them back. They waited for me at the bottom of the hill. We were left on our own. For work like that, Warden, plain physical stamina isn't enough. The lad stood it magnificently; I only just did. I think I was at the end of my tether. I must be getting old.'

They had unpacked the charges, one by one, and fixed them in position according to the destruction plan. They had to struggle every minute to avoid being swept away by the current. Clinging to each pile with their toes, they had to lower the plastic a sufficient depth into the water for it to be invisible, then mould it against the wood so that the explosive would act with maximum efficiency. Fumbling about underwater, they tied it on with those awful, prickly, searing ropes, which scored bloody furrows across their palms. The mere gesture of tightening the cords and tying the knots had become sheer torture. In the end they were forced to bob down and do it with their teeth.

This part of the operation had taken most of the night. The next task was less arduous, but more tricky. The detonators had been inserted at the same time as the charges were fixed. They now had to be linked together with a network of 'instantaneous' fuse, so that all the explosions would occur simultaneously. This is a job that demands a cool head, since a slip could cause a nasty mess. An explosives 'circuit' is much the same as an electric circuit, and each separate element has to be in its proper place. This was a fairly complicated one, for, in order to be on the safe side, Number One had doubled the number of fuse-lengths and detonators. These cords were fairly long, and the bits of iron which had been used to trim the raft had been fastened to them so as to make them sink.

'At last everything was ready. I don't think we did too badly. I thought I had better make a final inspection of the piles. It wasn't necessary. With Joyce, I needn't have worried. Nothing will shift out of place, I'm sure.'

They were worn out, bruised and battered, shivering

with cold, but they grew more and more exultant as they saw the end of their work in sight. They had dismantled the submarine and had let the bits of bamboo float off, one after the other. All that remained was to float downstream themselves, swimming towards the right bank, one carrying the battery in its waterproof case, the other paying out the wire which was weighted at intervals and kept afloat by the last hollow stick of bamboo. They had reached dry land at the spot they had reconnoitred. The bank there rose in a steep slope and the vegetation came down to the water's edge. They had camouflaged the wire in the undergrowth, and then hacked their way a dozen yards or so into the jungle. Joyce had set up the battery and generator.

'Over there, behind that red-coloured tree with its branches trailing in the water. I'm sure that's it,' Shears repeated.

'Everything seems to be under control,' said Warden. 'To-day's nearly over and he hasn't been discovered. We should have seen from here. No one's been anywhere near him. There's not much going on in camp itself, either. The prisoners left yesterday.'

'The prisoners left yesterday?'

'I saw quite a large column leaving camp. That party must have been to celebrate the end of their tasks, and the Japs obviously don't want to keep a lot of men hanging about here doing nothing.'

'That makes things still better.'

'There were a few who stayed behind. Casualties, I suppose, who weren't able to walk. So you left him over there, did you, Shears?'

'I left him over there. There was nothing more I could do and it was nearly dawn. I hope to God no one gets wind of him.'

'He's got his knife,' said Warden. 'Everything's working out perfectly. It's getting dark now. The Kwai valley is already in shadow. There's no chance of anything happening now.'

'There's always a chance of something happening when you least expect it, Warden. You know that as well as I do.

I don't know exactly why it is, but I've never yet come across a single instance of things going according to plan.'

'That's true. I've noticed that myself.'

'I wonder what we should expect to happen this time. When I left him, I still had a little bag of rice and a flask of whisky on me—the last of our provisions, which I had been carrying as carefully as the detonators. We drank a mouthful each and I left him the rest. He assured me for the last time that he felt perfectly confident. I left him there on his own.'

IV

Shears listened to the constant murmur of the River Kwai echoing through the jungles of Siam, and felt strangely perturbed.

He was now quite familiar with this ceaseless accompaniment to his every thought and gesture, yet this morning he was unable to recognise either its rhythm or volume. He stood motionless and uneasy for some time, all his faculties on the alert. Gradually he became aware, without being able to define it, of something unaccountably strange in the actual physical surroundings.

It seemed to him that in these surroundings (which were part and parcel of his very being) some transformation had taken place during his one night in the water and his one day spent on top of the mountain. The first sign of it had been his feeling, shortly before dawn, of inexplicable surprise. This had been followed by an odd impression of uneasiness which had gradually seeped up through his subconscious and developed into an actual thought—vague at first, but desperately struggling to express itself in more precise terms. Now, at sunrise, he was still unable to put it more clearly than in these words: 'Some change has occurred in the atmosphere round the bridge and above the river.'

'Something has changed . . .' He whispered the words over and over again. His special sense of 'atmosphere' hardly ever deceived him. His uneasiness developed into real anxiety, which he tried to dispel by logical argument. 'Of course, there's been a change. It's perfectly natural. Sound varies, depending on the place from where you listen. Here, I'm in the forest, at the foot of the mountain. The echo is not the same as on a hill-top or on the water. If this job lasts much longer, I'll end up by hearing things . . .'

He looked through the branches, but noticed nothing unusual. The river was barely visible in the dawn light. The opposite bank was still nothing but a solid grey mass. He forced himself to concentrate exclusively on the plan of battle and the disposition of the various groups waiting to go into action. Zero hour was not far off. He and four partisans had climbed down from the O.P. during the night. They had settled into positions chosen by Warden, close to the railway line and just above it. Warden himself and two other Siamese had stayed with the mortar. From up there he would be able to command the whole theatre of operations and be ready also to lend a hand after the attack. That was Number One's decision. He had told his friend that they had to have a European in command at each important post, to act on his own initiative if necessary. It was impossible to foresee everything or to give detailed orders in advance. Warden had understood. As for the third, the most important member of the team, the whole operation depended on him. Joyce had now been over there, exactly opposite Shears, for over twenty-four hours. He was waiting for the train. The convoy had left Bangkok during the night. A signal had reported its departure.

'Something's changed in the atmosphere . . .' Now the Siamese with the light machine-gun was also showing signs of alarm. He was squatting on his haunches, looking at the river.

Shears could not get rid of his feeling of uneasiness. The vague thought was still struggling to express itself more clearly, yet still defied analysis. Shears's brain was intent on solving this exasperating mystery.

The sound, he could swear, was now no longer the same.

A man with Shears's training was quick to note the symphony of the natural elements; he recorded it instinctively. This ability had served him well on two or three previous occasions. The shimmering eddy, the particular gurgling sound of water rushing over sand, the creak of branches bending with the current, all these this morning formed part of a different, less noisy concert—certainly less noisy than last night's. Shears seriously wondered if he was not going deaf. Or perhaps his nerves were not quite so steady?

But the Siamese could not have gone deaf at the same time. There was something else. All of a sudden another aspect of his impression flashed through his mind. There was a different smell as well. The smell of the River Kwai this morning was not the same as it had been. An oozy, dank miasma predominated, like the exhalation from a mud flat.

'River Kwai down!' the Siamese suddenly exclaimed.

And as the light began to reveal the details of the opposite bank, Shears suddenly realised. The tree, the big red tree where Joyce was hiding up, no longer had its branches trailing in the water. The River Kwai had sunk. The level had fallen during the night. How far? A foot perhaps? In front of the tree, at the bottom of the bank, there was now a pebbly beach still sparkling with water and shining in the rising sun.

The moment he realised this, Shears felt relieved to have found the explanation for his uneasiness and regained confidence in his nerves. His instinct had not let him down. He was not yet going mad. The eddies were no longer the same, neither those in the water nor those in the air above. It was really the whole atmosphere that had become affected. Newly-exposed earth, still wet, explained that dank smell.

Disaster never makes itself felt at once. The mind's natural inertia enforces a delay. Shears realised the fatal implications of this commonplace occurrence, one by one.

The River Kwai had sunk. In front of the red tree could be seen a broad flat area, which yesterday had been under water. The wire—the electric wire! Shears uttered an obscene oath. He took out his field-glasses and anxiously scanned the area of solid ground which had emerged during the night.

There was the wire. A long piece of it was now high and dry. Shears scanned it all the way from the water's edge up to the bank: a dark line dotted here and there with tufts of grass swept up by the current.

All the same, it was not too noticeable. Shears had managed to see it because he was looking for it. It could pass unnoticed if a Jap happened to come along that way. But the bank which previously had been inaccessible! There was now an unbroken beach at the foot of the slope, which stretched perhaps as far as the bridge (from here the bridge was out of sight) and which, to Shears's agonised glance, seemed designed to attract the attention of any passer-by. Still, while waiting for the train, the Japs were bound to be engaged on duties which would prevent them from sauntering along the river. Shears wiped his brow.

An operation never takes place exactly according to plan. At the last moment there is always some small, trivial, sometimes grotesque, occurrence which upsets the most carefully-worked-out programme. Number One blamed himself, as though he was personally responsible, for his negligence in failing to foresee the fall of the river. Of all nights, it had to happen now—not one night later, nor two nights earlier!

That open beach without a blade of grass on it, lying naked, as naked as truth itself, absorbed his whole attention. The river must have sunk considerably. By a foot? By two feet? Perhaps more? Oh God!

Shears suddenly felt faint. He clung to a tree to prevent the Siamese from seeing how his limbs were trembling. This was the second time in his life that he had felt so upset. The first was when he had felt an enemy's blood trickling through his fingers. His heart literally, actually, stopped beating and his whole body broke out in a cold sweat.

By two feet? Perhaps more? God Almighty! The charges! The charges of plastic on the piles of the bridge!

V

After Shears had shaken his hand and left him alone in the hide-out, Joyce had felt completely fuddled for some time. The realisation that he now had no one to rely on but himself went to his head like fumes of alcohol. He was physically insensible to the fatigue of the previous night and the clammy discomfort of his sodden clothes. He was not yet conscious of that feeling of power and conquest which absolute isolation affords, whether on a mountain-top or in the bowels of the earth.

When his head cleared, he had to reason with himself before he could finally decide to take certain necessary steps before dawn so as to avoid giving in to his lassitude. If this decision had not entered his head he would have stayed there without moving, leaning against a tree, his hand on the plunger, gazing at the bridge whose dark shape could be seen, outlined against a corner of starlit sky above the thick mass of low bushes, through the less thick foliage of taller trees. He had instinctively adopted this position as soon as Shears left.

He got up, took off his clothes, wrung them out and massaged his frozen limbs. He put his shorts and shirt on again; although still wet, they were some defence against the chilly early-morning air. He ate as much as he could of the rice that Shears had left him, then took a long swig of whisky. He felt it was too late now to leave his hide-out to go and fetch some water. He used some of the spirit to wash the wounds which speckled his limbs. He sat down again at the foot of the tree and waited. Nothing happened that day. He had not expected anything to happen. The train was not due until the morning; but he felt more able to dictate the course of events by being here on the spot.

Several times he saw some Japanese on the bridge. They obviously suspected nothing and no one looked in his direc-tion. As in his dream, he had picked out an easily distinguishable landmark on the platform, a cross-beam of the parapet which was in line with himself and a dead branch. This was exactly half-way across, that is to say at one end of the 'prepared' section of piles. When the engine reached it, or rather when it was still a few feet off, he would apply his full weight to the plunger. With the picture of an imaginary engine in his mind, he had disconnected the wire and practised this simple gesture twenty times over, so as to make it an automatic reaction. The machine was in perfect working order. He had carefully dried it and wiped it clean, conscientiously removing the slightest blemish. His own reflexes were also working well.

The day went by quite quickly. When it was dark he scrambled down the slope, swallowed several mouthfuls of muddy water, filled his bottle, then returned to his hide-out. He allowed himself to doze leaning against a tree, without shifting his position. If, for some extraordinary reason, the train's schedule were to be changed, he would still be able to hear it in the distance, he felt certain. When one has lived for some time in the jungle, one quickly develops the instinctive wariness of a wild beast.

He slept by fits and starts, punctuated by long bouts of insomnia. In between, visions of his present adventure alternated strangely with memories of that past life of his which he had described to Shears before launching out on the river.

He was once again in the dusty workroom in which some of the best years of his life had been spent sitting day after day and for long gloomy hours in front of a sheet of drawing-paper under a projector-lamp. The girder, that bit of metal which he had never actually seen, was responsible for the mathematical symbols in two dimensions which had occupied the whole of his youth. The plan, the outline, the elevation and countless cross-sections came to life before his very eyes, with all the details of the structure on which a staff of experts had managed to achieve a saving of a pound and a half of steel after two years of tests and experiments.

Superimposed on this picture, against the background of

this structure, were the small brown squares, like those Warden had drawn, fixed to the twenty-four piles on the large-scale plan of the bridge. The heading, over which he had sweated so painfully and so many times, the final heading came into focus, then grew blurred as he watched it. He tried in vain to decipher the letters. They were dotted all over his drawing-paper, until at last they fused together again, as sometimes happens at the end of a film on a cinema screen, to form a single word. It was the word DESTRUCTION, in heavy black letters written in shiny ink, which reflected the light of the projector-lamp and bewilderingly filled the whole screen, leaving no room for any other character.

He was not really obsessed by this sight. He could avoid it whenever he wanted. All he had to do was open his eyes. The dark corner in which the River Kwai bridge stood outlined in black banished these dusty ghosts of the past and summoned him back to reality; his present reality. His life would no longer be the same after this. He was already tasting the fruits of success while witnessing his own metamorphosis.

At first light, about the same time as Shears, he too felt uneasy on account of the perceptible change in the emanations from the river. The alteration had been so gradual that in his fuddled state he had not even been aware of it. From his hide-out he could see only the platform of the bridge. The river was out of sight, but he was certain his feelings were justified. This certainty soon became so overwhelming that he felt he could no longer remain inactive. He pushed his way through the undergrowth towards the river, reached the last curtain of branches and looked out. He saw the reason for his uneasiness at the same time that he noticed the electric wire lying exposed on the pebble beach.

Following the same course as Shears, his mind slowly grasped the significance of this irreparable disaster. In the same way he felt his whole body quiver at the thought of the plastic charges. From his new position he would be able to see the piles. He had only to raise his eyes. He forced himself to do so.

It took him a fairly long time to appreciate how much the risk had been increased by the River Kwai's whimsical behaviour. Even after close observation he could not assess the extent with any degree of accuracy, but oscillated between hope and despair at each of the thousand ripples which the current created round the bridge. At first glance a wave of voluptuous optimism eased his nerves, which were tense with the horror of his original fears. The river had not sunk so very much. The charges were still under water.

At least they seemed to be, from this position rather far down. But from above? From the bridge? And even from here? Concentrating still more closely, he now noticed a fairly large wave, like one created by a flow of water round a grounded wreck, washing round the piles, those piles which he knew so well and which he had left encrusted with strips of his own flesh. The waves round those particular piles were larger than the rest. And on one of them he thought he could see a patch of brown against the lighter colour of the wood. This emerged from time to time like a fish's dorsal fin, yet a moment later there was nothing to be seen but the eddy. The charge was probably just below the surface of the water. A keen sentry would certainly be able to spot those on the outside rows simply by leaning over the parapet.

And what if the level should fall still further? In a moment, perhaps, the charges would be visible for all to see, still dripping with water, sparkling in the harsh light of the Siamese sun! He was numbed by the grotesque absurdity of the picture. What time was it? How long would it take? The sun was just beginning to light up the valley. The train was not due before ten o'clock. Their patience, their toil, their anxiety, their suffering, all had suddenly been rendered pitiful and almost ludicrous by the inhuman whim of this trickle from the mountains. The success of the big attack, for which he had for good and all sacrificed his hitherto neglected reserves of stamina and strength after thriftily saving them up for years, was now again in the balance. being weighed once more on scales which took no heed of his soul's ambition. His destiny was to be fulfilled during the minutes that remained before the train's arrival, fulfilled regardless of himself, fulfilled on a higher plane; consciously fulfilled, perhaps, but in an external consciousness, a pitiless consciousness scornful of the impulse which had carried him thus far, a consciousness which directed human affairs at such a high level that no human wish could sway it, neither entreaty nor despair.

This feeling that the discovery or non-discovery of the explosive was now independent of anything he could do made him, paradoxically enough, a little calmer. He stopped thinking about it, and even stopped hoping. He could not afford to waste an ounce of energy on things that were taking place on a supernatural plane. He had to forget about them, so as to concentrate all his resources on the factors which were still within the scope of his own initiative. It was on these, and these alone, that he now had to bring his mind to bear. The operation was still feasible; he only had to envisage what form it was likely to take. He was still wondering what his reactions would be. Shears had noticed him doing that before.

If the charges were discovered, the train would be stopped before it reached the bridge. He would then thrust plunger down before being discovered himself. The damage would be easily repaired. It would be only a partial success, but he could not help that.

It was a different situation when it came to the electric wire. This could be seen by anyone walking along the beach a few feet away from him. In that case there was still a chance of taking independent action. Perhaps there would be no one on the bridge at that moment, and no one on the opposite bank who could see him. And the slope hid the pebble beach from the Japanese in the camp. The man would probably hesitate before sounding the alarm. In that case he, Joyce, would have to act, and act fast. And to do that, he would have to keep both bridge and beach in view.

He thought again, returned to his previous hide-out and

brought his gear back to the new position behind a flimsy screen of undergrowth from which he could see at the same time the bridge and the patch of open ground now bisected by the wire. An idea crossed his mind. He took off his shirt and shorts. He kept on his pants. This was more or less like the prisoners' working kit. From a long way off he might be mistaken for one of them. He carefully set up the generator and knelt down beside it. He took his knife out of its sheath. This important item of equipment, which was included on every Plastic and Destructions Company expedition, he placed on the grass by his side. Then he waited.

The time passed desperately slowly, at a snail's pace, as sluggishly as the diminished flow of the River Kwai; it was measured for him in endless seconds by the muffled murmur of the water nibbling imperceptibly into a future fraught with danger, storing up in the past a few flashes of security, each invaluable but infinitesimal and tragically out of proportion with his anxiety. The tropical light flooded the dripping valley and shimmered on the wet black sand of the recently exposed river bed. After outlining the cross-beams in the superstructure of the bridge, the sun, hidden for a moment by the platform, rose above this obstruction, casting before it the gigantic shadow of this example of human artifice. It crossed the pebble beach in a straight line parallel to the wire, was distorted in the water where it writhed in countless curves, then melted away on the other side into the shape of the hills beyond. The heat hardened the cuts on his tattered hands and made the wounds on his body smart horribly in the grip of multi-coloured legions of ants. But physical pain did not distract his thoughts; it was only an agonising accompaniment to the obsession which had been wracking his brain for the last few minutes.

A fresh fear had assailed him just as he was trying to imagine what form the action would have to take if, during the next few hours, his fate-line were to be crossed by one particular event— a Japanese soldier wandering idly along the river and stopping to investigate the pebble beach. He would be surprised to see the wire. He would stop. He would bend down to take hold of it and stand still for a moment. It was then that he, Joyce, would have to intervene. It was essential for him to visualise his own actions in advance. As Shears had said, he brooded too much!

Picturing this action was enough to tie his nerves in knots and paralyse every muscle. He could not help it. He had a deep instinctive feeling that this action was imperative, that it had been ordained a long time ago, that it was the natural conclusion of events leading inevitably to this final test of his capabilities. It was the most dreaded, hateful test of all, which he could throw on to one or the other side of the scales, a test sufficiently fraught with horror and sacrifice by itself to tip the scales on the side of success by snatching him from the hungry grasp of destiny.

He exercised all his brain cells with this final end in view, feverishly going over in his mind the school instructions, trying to devote himself body and soul to the dynamics of the job on hand, yet still unable to banish the nightmare of the immediate consequences.

He remembered the worrying question which his C.O. had once asked him: 'When the time comes, would you be "capable," in cold blood, of using this weapon?' He had been uneasy about his instinctive reactions and will-power. He had not been able to give a definite answer. At the moment of launching out on the river he had been absolutely certain; now he was not sure of anything. He looked at the weapon lying on the grass beside him.

It was a sharp long-bladed knife with a short metal hilt just big enough to ensure a reasonable grip, blade and hilt being all in one piece. The backroom boys of Force 316 had modified its blade and handle several times. The instructions in its use had been specific. It was not simply a question of clenching one's fist round it and striking blindly; that was too easy; anyone could do that. Every form of destruction requires its own individual technique. The instructors had taught him two methods of using it. For purposes of defence, against a man rushing forward, it was advisable to hold it in front of one, with the point tilted slightly upwards and the cutting edge uppermost, and to strike with an upward thrust as though disembowelling an animal. The gesture itself was not beyond his powers. He could have done it almost automatically. But in this case he would not have to There would be no enemy rushing forward. He would not have to defend himself. For the action which he was anticipating, he would have to use the second method. It needed hardly any strength, but a lot of skill and utter ruthlessness. It was the method by which the trainees were taught to wipe out a sentry in the dark without giving him the time or opportunity to raise the alarm. It necessitated striking from behind; but not in the man's back (that, too, would have been too easy). It necessitated cutting his throat.

The knife had to be held palm downwards, with the nails underneath, the thumb running along the root of the blade to ensure proper control; with the blade itself held horizontal and perpendicular to the victim's body. The thrust had to be made from right to left, firmly but not violently enough to turn it off its course, and directed at a certain point an inch or two below the ear. This point and no other had to be aimed at and hit, to prevent the man from crying out. Such was the general plan of the operation. It also involved several further subsidiary gestures secondary but no less important, which had to be carried out immediately after the blade's penetration. But the advice on this subject, which the Calcutta instructors gave so light-heartedly, Joyce did not even dare whisper to himself.

He could not dispel his mental picture of the immediate consequences. So he forced himself instead to examine it closely, to build it up in his mind in every detail of its shape and horrid colour. He made himself analyse its most frightening aspects, in the mad hope that he would thereby get used to it and so reach that state of detachment which is born of habit. He relived the scene a dozen times, twenty times over, and gradually managed to create not a ghost, nor even a vague imaginary shadow, but a human being, a real flesh and blood Japanese soldier standing on the beach in uniform, wearing his funny cap, his ear projecting underneath it, and a little lower down the small patch of brown skin which he aimed at as he silently lifted his outstretched arm. He forced himself to feel, to judge the resistance to the blow, to see the blood spurting and the body jerking as the knife in the palm of his clenched fist went through the subsidiary gestures and his left arm flashed down and bared the victim's throat. He steeped himself for hour after hour in the worst horror he could imagine. He made such an effort to train his body to be nothing more than an insensible obedient machine that he felt overwhelming fatigue in every muscle.

He was still not sure of himself. He was appalled to see that this method of preparing himself was not effective. The threat of failure taunted him as relentlessly as the realisation of his duty. He had to choose between two courses: the first ignominiously scattering, in an eternity of shame and remorse, the same horror that the second concentrated in a few seconds of ghastly action—an ignominious but passive course, demanding only inactive cowardice and so all the more attractive for providing the insidious temptation of the easy way out. He came to realise that in cold blood and in full possession of his faculties he would never be capable of the action which he insisted on picturing to himself. He felt, on the contrary, that he would have to banish it from his mind and find either a stimulating or sobering alternative which would turn his thoughts elsewhere. He needed more help than he could derive from the paralysing contemplation of this terrifying task.

Outside help. He looked round him in despair. He was alone and naked in a strange land, skulking in the undergrowth like a wild beast, surrounded by enemies of every kind. His only weapon was this dreadful dagger burning a hole in the palm of his hand. He searched in vain for some support from any feature in the landscape which had fired his imagination. Everything now looked hostile in the Kwai valley. The shadow of the bridge faded as the minutes went by. The bridge was now nothing but a lifeless, useless structure. There was no hope of help. He had nothing more to drink, nothing to eat. It might have been comforting to gulp down some sort of food, any sort.

He could expect no outside help. He was left entirely to his own devices. This was what he had wanted, what he had welcomed. He had felt proud and inspired. His personal powers had seemed invincible. Surely they could not all of a sudden fade away, leaving him stranded like some machine with a sabotaged engine! He closed his eyes on the surrounding world and looked inwards on himself. If there was any hope of rescue it lay there, and not on this earth beneath these skies. In his present misery the only gleam of hope he could see was the hypnotising flame of those mental pictures which are born of hallucination. His imagination was his only refuge. Shears had been worried by that. Warden had wisely not declared whether it was a virtue or a fault.

He had to combat the evil effects of obsession by the counter-poison of self-imposed obsession; to unwind the film on which the representative symbols of his spiritual capital were inscribed; to examine with an inquisitor's fury every spectre in his mental universe; to hunt passionately through these immaterial witnesses of his existence until he found a sufficiently absorbing figure to occupy the whole realm of his consciousness without leaving a single gap. Feverishly he reviewed them all. Hatred of the Japanese, sense of duty—these were ludicrous irritants which could not be expressed in a sufficiently clear form. He thought of his superior officers, of his friends who were relying on him entirely and who were now waiting on the opposite bank. Even that thought was not sufficiently real. It was barely sufficient to induce him to sacrifice his own life. Even the intoxication of success was now of no avail. Or else he would have to envisage victory under a more palpable guise than that half-extinguished halo of glory whose fading beams could no longer find any material element on which to shine.

A thought suddenly flashed through his mind. It flashed with startling clarity for a split second. Even before realising it, he had the feeling that it was sufficiently significant to give him hope. He struggled to retrieve it. It flashed again. It was last night's vision: the sheet of drawing-paper under the projector-lamp; the countless designs for the girder on which the brown squares were superimposed and which were dwarfed by a heading endlessly repeated in huge shining letters: the word DESTRUCTION.

It went on flashing. From the moment that it was instinctively recalled and triumphantly occupied his thoughts, he felt that this alone was sufficiently consistent, sufficiently complete, sufficiently powerful to make him rise above the disgust and horror of his wretched carcase. It was as exhilarating as drink and as soothing as opium. He gave in to it completely and took care not to let it escape him again.

Having reached this state of self-induced hypnosis, he was not surprised to see some Japanese soldiers walking along the bridge over the River Kwai.

VI

Shears also saw the Japanese soldiers, and lived through another nightmare.

For him, too, time was passing at a relentlessly slow pace. After the dismay caused by the thought of the charges, he had pulled himself together. He had left the partisans in position, and climbed a little further up the slope. He had stopped at a point from which he could see the bridge as well as the river. He had noticed the little waves round the piles and examined them through his field-glasses. He imagined he could see a patch of brown rising and falling with the movement of the eddies. Instinctively, involuntarily, and from a sense of duty, he had wracked his brains to discover what personal action he could take to avert this stroke of misfortune. 'There is always something further to be done, some extra action to take,' so the Force 316 authorities asserted. For the first time since he had been engaged on this sort of work Shears could think of nothing to do, and he cursed himself for his impotence.

For him the die was cast. He had no more chance of retaliating than had Warden, who from up there had no doubt also discovered the treachery of the River Kwai. Joyce perhaps? But had he even noticed the change? And who could tell if he would have the necessary initiative and instinct to deal with such a catastrophe? Shears, who was used to judging the size of the obstacle to be overcome in situations of this sort, bitterly regretted not having taken his place.

Two endless hours had dragged by. From the spot he had reached he could see the hutments of the camp. He had noticed some Japanese soldiers moving about in full-dress uniform. A hundred yards away from the river there was a whole company of them waiting for the train, lined up in honour of the authorities who were to open the railway line. Perhaps the preparations for this ceremony would occupy all their attention? Shears hoped so. But a Japanese patrol had emerged from the guardroom and was now on its way to the bridge.

Now the men, led by a sergeant, were moving along the platform in two ranks, one on either side of the track. They walked slowly along in a rather dreamy manner, their rifles carried carelessly at the slope. Their mission was to make a final inspection before the train arrived. From time to time one of them stopped to lean over the parapet. Clearly it was only to salve their conscience, to carry out their orders, that they were performing this task. Shears tried to persuade himself that their hearts were not in the job— which was probably true. No accident could happen to the bridge over the River Kwai whose growth in this God-forsaken valley they had personally witnessed day by day! 'They're looking without seeing,' he told himself as he watched them advance. Each step they took echoed through his head. He forced himself to keep his eyes on them and follow every movement they made, while he silently delivered a vague prayer to whatever god or devil or other mysterious power there might be. He automatically judged their speed and the distance they moved along the bridge in every second. They were now more than half-way across. The sergeant leaned over the parapet and spoke to the leading man, pointing at the river. Shears bit his hand to keep himself from shouting out loud. The sergeant laughed. He was probably making some remark about the fall in the level of the water. They moved off again. Shears was right: they were looking without seeing. He felt that by following them like this with his eyes, he would be able to exercise an influence on their sense of perception—a miracle of telepathic suggestion. The last man had gone past. They had noticed nothing.

Now they were coming back. They were moving along the bridge in the opposite direction at the same ambling pace. One of them leaned head and shoulders right over the dangerous section, then stepped back into the ranks.

They had gone past again. Shears mopped his brow. They were moving away. 'They have seen nothing'; automatically he whispered these words to himself, to convince himself all the more of the miracle. Anxiously he kept them under observation and did not take his eyes off them until they had rejoined the company. Before allowing his hopes to soar he was seized by a strange feeling of pride.

'If I'd been one of them,' he muttered, 'I shouldn't have been so careless. Any British soldier would have spotted the sabotage. Ah well, the train won't be long now.'

As though in answer to this last thought, he heard a harsh voice shouting out orders on the enemy bank. There was a stir among the men. Shears looked into the distance. On the horizon of the plain a small cloud of black smoke proclaimed the approach of the first Japanese convoy to cross into Siam, the first train, loaded with troops, munitions and high-ranking Japanese generals, which was about to cross the bridge over the River Kwai.

Shears's heart softened. Tears of gratitude to the mysterious power ran down his cheeks.

'Nothing can stop us now,' he whispered. 'Fate has no more tricks to play. The train will be here in twenty minutes.'

He quelled his anxiety and returned to the foot of the mountain in order to take command of the support group. As he scrambled down, bent double and taking care to keep under cover, he was unable to see the fine upstanding officer in the uniform of a British colonel approaching the bridge from the opposite bank.

At the very moment that Number One got back in position, still in a flurry of emotion, with every faculty concentrated on the anticipated sight of a blinding explosion followed by the fire and wreckage that spell success, Colonel Nicholson in his turn started to cross the bridge over the River Kwai.

With a clear conscience, at peace with the universe and with God, gazing through eyes that are bluer than the tropical sky after a storm, feeling through every pore of his ruddy skin the satisfaction of the well-earned rest that is due to any craftsman after a difficult task, proud of having overcome every obstacle through his personal courage and perseverance, glorying in the work accomplished by himself and by his men in this corner of Siam which he now feels almost belongs to him, light at heart at the thought of having shown himself worthy of his forefathers and of having contributed a far from common chapter to the eastern legends of empire-builders, firmly convinced that no one could have done the job better, confirmed in his certainty of the superiority of his own race in every field of activity, glad of having furnished ample proof of this during the last six months, bursting with the joy that makes every commander's effort worth while once the triumphant result is there for all to see, drinking the cup of victory in tiny sips, delighted with the quality of the construction, anxious to see for himself, and for the last time, the sum total of its perfection compounded of hard work and intelligence, and also in order to carry out a final inspection, Colonel Nicholson strode with dignity across the bridge over the River Kwai.

Most of the prisoners, and all the officers, had left two days before, on foot, for an assembly point from which they were due to be sent to Malaya, to the islands or to Japan, in order to undertake other duties. The railway was finished. The ceremony which His Imperial Majesty in Tokyo had graciously ordained, and imposed, on all the groups in Burma and Siam, had been held in honour of its completion.

It had been celebrated with particular pomp in the River Kwai camp. Colonel Nicholson had seen to that. All along the line it had been preceded by the usual speeches from Japanese officers, generals and colonels, perched on a rostrum, wearing black boots and grey gloves, gesticulating with their arms and heads, making an extraordinary parody of the language of the Western world in front of a legion of white men, men who were crippled, sick and covered in sores and still in a daze after living through several months of hell.

Saito had spoken a few words, of course, in praise of the South-East Asia Sphere, and had condescended to add his thanks for the loyalty which the prisoners had shown. Clipton, whose temper had been sorely tried for weeks, during which he had seen dying men dragging themselves to the workyards in order to finish the bridge, felt almost like weeping with rage. He had then had to put up with a short speech from Colonel Nicholson, in which the C.O. congratulated his men, extolling their self-sacrifice and fortitude. The Colonel had ended up by declaring that their hardships had not been suffered in vain and that he was proud of being in command of such fine fellows. Their conduct and demeanour in the face of adversity would be an example to the whole country.

After that came the festivities. The Colonel had lent a hand and taken an active part in them. He knew that nothing was worse for the men than inactivity, and had ordered a mass of entertainments, the organisation of which had kept them breathless for several days. There were not only several concerts, but also a comic turn performed by soldiers in fancy dress, and even a ballet of men made up as dancers which provoked a hearty laugh.

'You see, Clipton,' he had said, 'you criticised me once, but I stuck to my guns. I've kept the morale of the unit high, and that's the main thing. The men have stuck it out.'

This was true. A fine spirit had been maintained in the River Kwai camp. Clipton had to admit this when he looked

at the men round him. It was obvious that they were taking
an innocent, childish pleasure in these celebrations, and the
sincerity of their cheers left no room for doubt about the
level of their morale.

The next day the prisoners had moved off. Only the seriously ill and the cripples had stayed behind. They were to
be evacuated to Bangkok in the next train from Burma.
The officers had left with the men. Reeves and Hughes, to
their great regret, had been obliged to join the convoy and
had not been allowed to see the first train cross the construction which had cost them so much toil and effort.
Colonel Nicholson, however, had been given permission to
travel with the sick men. Because of the services he had
rendered, Saito had not been able to refuse him this favour,
which he had requested in his usual dignified manner.

He now walked along, taking lengthy brisk strides which
resounded triumphantly on the platform. He had won the
day. The bridge was ready. There was nothing fancy about
it, but it was a sufficiently 'finished' job to advertise the
qualities of the Western world in large letters across this
Siamese sky. This was where he deserved to be, in the position of a commander reviewing his troops before a victorious march-past. It was unthinkable that he should be
elsewhere. His presence was some consolation for the departure of his faithful assistants and his men, all of whom
deserved to share in this honour. Luckily he at least was
here. The bridge was soundly built, he knew. There was no
weak spot. It would stand up to what was expected of it.
But nothing can take the place of a final examination by
the man responsible for it, of that he was also certain. One
can never foresee every eventuality. Years of experience had
taught him that something always tends to crop up at the
last moment, that there is always some fly in the ointment.
If it does, even the best junior officer is incapable of taking
the necessary steps to deal with it. Needless to say, he placed
no faith in the report made by the Japanese patrol which
Saito had sent out that morning. He had to see to things
himself. As he strode along, his glance confirmed the firm-
ness of each support and the soundness of each joint.

When he was a little over half-way across he leant over the parapet, as he had done every five or six yards on the way. He caught sight of a pile and stood rooted to the spot with surprise.

His trained eye had at once noticed the extra ripples on the surface of the water caused by one of the charges. Examining them more closely, Colonel Nicholson thought he saw a brown patch against the wood. He hesitated for a moment, then moved on and stopped a few yards further off, above another pile. Once again he leant over the parapet.

'That's funny,' he muttered.

Again he hesitated, then crossed the line and looked over the other side. Another patch of brown was visible a bare inch below the surface. This made him feel vaguely annoyed, like the sight of a blot disfiguring his work. He decided to walk on, went as far as the end of the platform, turned round and retraced his steps, as the patrol had done before him, then stopped once more, wrapped in thought and shaking his head. Finally he shrugged his shoulders and turned towards the right bank. He kept talking to himself the whole time.

'That wasn't there two days ago,' he mumbled. 'The water level was higher, it's true. Probably some muck that's been washed up against the piles and stuck there. Yet . . .'

The ghost of a suspicion flashed through his mind, but the truth was too extraordinary for him to grasp it immediately. Yet he was no longer in a cheerful mood. His morning was spoilt. He turned round again to have another look at the anomaly, found no explanation, and finally stepped off the bridge still feeling rather puzzled.

'It can't be true,' he muttered, as he contemplated the vague suspicion skimming through his brain. 'Unless it's one of those Chinese Communists bands . . .'

Sabotage was firmly associated in his mind with gangster activity.

'It can't be true,' he repeated, still unable to recapture his light-hearted mood.

The train was now in sight, though still some way off, struggling up the line. The Colonel calculated that it would take at least ten minutes to arrive. Saito, who was strolling up and down between the bridge and the company, watched him approach and felt embarrassed as he always did in the Englishman's presence. Colonel Nicholson suddenly made up his mind as he drew level with the Japanese.

'Colonel Saito,' he declared in a lordly manner, 'there's something rather odd going on. We'd better look into it more closely before the train goes across.'

Without waiting for an answer, he scrambled quickly down the slope. His intention was to take the small native canoe moored under the bridge and make a tour of inspection round the piles. As he reached the beach he instinctively swept it with his trained glance and noticed the length of electric wire on the shining pebbles. Colonel Nicholson frowned and walked over towards it.

VII

It was while he was scrambling down the slope with an ease born of the daily habit of light exercise and the peaceful contemplation of everyday truths, that he came into Shears's field of view. The Japanese colonel followed close behind him. It was only then that Shears realised that adversity still had a card up its sleeve. Joyce had been aware of this for some time. In the state of trance to which he had managed to force himself he had seen the Colonel's behaviour on the bridge without any further feeling of alarm. But he seized his dagger as soon as he saw the figure of Saito following behind him on the beach.

Shears noticed that as Colonel Nicholson approached he seemed to be dragging the Japanese officer along in his wake. In face of this incoherent situation he felt himself give way to a sort of hysteria; he began babbling to himself:

'But the other fellow's leading him to it! It's our own

colonel who's taking him there! If only I could explain, have a word with him, just a word!'

The sound of the puffing engine could be heard in the distance. All the Japanese were probably now on parade, ready to present arms. The two men on the beach were invisible from the camp. Number One made an angry gesture as he instantly grasped the whole situation and instinctively realised what action would have to be taken, the action which a situation of this sort required and demanded of every man who had enlistened in the ranks of the Plastic and Destructions Company. He too seized his knife. He tore it out of his belt and held it in front of him according to the school training, palm downwards, the nails underneath, the thumb running along the root of the blade—not in order to use it, but in the wild hope that he would be able to influence Joyce by suggestion, and moved by the same instinct which had induced him a little earlier to follow the movements of the patrol.

Colonel Nicholson had stopped in front of the wire. Saito was coming up behind him, waddling along on his stumpy legs. All the emotions that Shears had felt in the morning were nothing to what he felt at that moment. He began talking out loud, brandishing the dagger in front of him above his head.

'He won't be able to do it! There's a limit to what you can expect of a lad of that age who's been brought up in the ordinary way and spent his whole life in an office. I was made to let him have his way. It was up to me to take his place. He won't be able to do it!'

Saito had caught up with Colonel Nicholson, who had bent down and picked up the wire. Shears felt his heart thumping against his ribs.

'He won't be able to do it! Three minutes more, just three minutes, and the train will be here. He won't be able to do it!',

One of the Siamese partisans crouching by his rifle gazed at him in terror. Luckily the jungle muffled the sound of his voice. He was hunched up, clenching his fist round the knife which he held motionless in front of him.

'He won't be able to do it! God Almighty, make him lose his head; make him fighting mad—just for ten seconds!'

As he uttered this wild prayer, he noticed a movement in the undergrowth, and the bushes parted. He stiffened and held his breath. Joyce was silently creeping down the slope, bent double, with his knife in his hand. Shears fastened his eyes on him, and kept them there.

Saito, whose mind worked slowly, was crouching at the water's edge with his back to the forest, in the Oriental's favourite position which he instinctively adopted whenever any unforeseen event made him forget to guard himself against it. He too had picked up the wire. Shears heard a few words spoken in English :

'This is really rather alarming, Colonel Saito.'

After that there was a short silence. The Jap was pulling the strands apart in his fingers. Joyce had arrived unobserved behind the two men.

'My God,' the Colonel suddenly yelled, 'the bridge has been mined, Colonel Saito! Those damn things I saw against the piles were explosives! And this wire . . .'

He had turned round towards the jungle, while Saito let the weight of these words sink in. Shears watched still more intently. As his fist flashed across from right to left, he saw an answering flash on the opposite bank. He at once recognised the familiar change that had come over the man crouching there.

So he had been able to do it? He had done it. Not a muscle in his tensed body had faltered while the steel went in with hardly any resistance. He had gone through the subsidiary gestures without a tremor. And at that very moment, partly in order to obey the instructions he had received and partly because he felt the overwhelming need to cling to something human, he had brought his left fist down on to the neck of the enemy whose throat he had just slit. In his death-spasm Saito had begun to straighten his legs and was in a semi-upright position. Joyce had clasped him with all his strength against his own body, partly to stifle him and partly to still the trembling which had started in his own limbs.

The Jap had collapsed. He had not uttered a sound, apart from the death rattle, which Shears only heard because he was expecting it. For a few seconds Joyce lay paralysed underneath his adversary, who had fallen on top of him and was drenching him with his blood. He had had the strength to win the first round. Now he was not sure that he had enough will-power to struggle free. At last he gave a heave. In a single movement he threw off the lifeless body, which rolled half into the water, then looked round.

Both banks were deserted. He had won, but his pride could not dispel either his horror or disgust. With an effort he got up on to his hands and knees. There were still a few simple things he had to do. First of all, explain himself. Two words would be enough. Colonel Nicholson had remained rooted to the spot, petrified by the suddenness of the scene he had witnessed.

'Officer! British officer, sir!' Joyce muttered. 'The bridge is going up. Stand clear!'

He could not recognise his own voice. The effort of moving his lips caused him untold labour. Yet this fellow here did not even seem to hear him!

'British officer, sir!' he repeated in despair. 'Force 316 from Calcutta. Commandos. Orders to blow up the bridge.'

Colonel Nicholson at last showed some sign of life. A strange light sparkled in his eyes. He spoke in a hollow voice:

'Blow up the bridge?'

'Stand clear, sir. Here comes the train. They'll think you're in on it too.'

The Colonel still did not move.

This was no time for argument. He would have to act. The puffing of the engine could be heard quite distinctly. Joyce realised that his legs would not carry the weight of his body. On all fours he clambered up the slope, back to his position in the undergrowth.

'Blow up the bridge?' the Colonel repeated.

He had not moved an inch. He had blankly watched

Joyce's painful progress, as though trying to grasp the meaning of the words. Suddenly he moved and followed in his footsteps. He tore through the curtain of branches which had just closed behind him and stumbled on the hideout with the generator, on which he at once laid his hand.

'Blow up the bridge!' the Colonel once more exclaimed.

'British officer, sir!' Joyce stammered almost plaintively. 'British officer from Calcutta. Orders . . .'

He did not finish the sentence. Colonel Nicholson had launched himself at him with a yell:

'Help!'

VIII

'Two men lost. Some damage done but bridge intact thanks to British Colonel's heroism.'

Such was the concise report which Warden, the only survivor of the trio, sent to Calcutta on his return to base.

When he read this signal Colonel Green felt that there were a lot of points which needed clearing up in this strange business, and asked for an explanation. Warden replied that he had nothing further to say. His C.O. then decided that he had been long enough in the jungles of Siam and that a man could not be left on his own in that dangerous spot when the Japanese were probably going to search the area. At this stage of the war Force 316 was in a strong position. A second team was dropped on to a D.Z. some distance away to maintain contact with the Siamese, and Warden was recalled to H.Q. A submarine came to take him off from a secret beach in the Bay of Bengal, which he managed to reach after an eventful two weeks' march. Three days later he was in Calcutta and reported to Colonel Green.

He gave him a brief summary of the preparations for the attack, then came to the operation itself. From the top of the hill he had witnessed the whole scene; not a detail had escaped him. He began speaking in the cool, calculated tone which he normally used; but as he went on with his story his voice changed. During the last month that he had spent as the only white man surrounded by Siamese partisans a flood of unexpressed sensations had been surging through him. Each episode in the drama constantly recurred, bubbling through his brain, yet with his usual love of logic he instinctively struggled to find a rational explanation and to reduce them all to a handful of universal principles.

The outcome of these conflicting mental exercises came to light one day in the offices of Force 316. He had not been able to confine himself to a dry military report. He had felt an urgent need to unleash the storm of his fears and anxiety, his doubts and rage, and also to reveal quite candidly the reasons for the grotesque sequel in so far as he could fathom them. He was impelled by his sense of duty to give in addition a factual account of what had happened. He tried to stick to this and occasionally succeeded, only to give way again and again to the torrent of his uncontrollable temper. The result was a strange combination of almost incoherent invective mingled with the elements of an impassioned address, sprinkled here and there with extravagant contradictions and only an occasional 'fact.'

Colonel Green listened patiently and attentively to this piece of fantastic rhetoric, in which he could see no sign of the cool reasoning for which Professor Warden was famous. He was interested in facts more than anything else. But he interrupted the junior officer as little as possible. He had had some experience in dealing with men returning from similar missions, to which they had devoted themselves heart and soul only to see their efforts result in an ignominious failure for which they themselves were not responsible. In such cases he made a fairly liberal allowance for the 'human element,' closing his eyes to their aberrations and pretending to overlook the occasional lack of respect in their tone of voice.

'I suppose you'd say the lad behaved like a fool, sir. Well, yes, he did; but no one in his place could have done better. I watched him. I didn't take my eyes off him for a second. I could guess what he was saying to that colonel.

He did what I should have done in his place. I watched him as he dragged himself off. The train was almost there. I didn't know what was happening myself until the other fellow rushed at him. I only realised later, when I'd had time to think. And Shears claimed that he thought too much! My God, he didn't think too much; he didn't think enough! He should have been more perceptive, more discerning. Then he would have understood that in our job it's no good cutting any old throat. You've got to cut the right one. Isn't that so, sir?'

'More insight, that's what he needed; then he would have known who his enemy really was, realised it was that old brute who couldn't stand the idea of his fine work being destroyed. A really perceptive mind would have deduced that from the way he strode along the platform. I had my glasses trained on him, sir; if only it had been a rifle! He had the sanctimonious smile of a conqueror on his lips, I remember. A splendid example of the man of action, sir, as we say in Force 316. He never let misfortune get him down; always made a last effort. It was he who shouted to the Japs for help!

'That old brute with his blue eyes had probably spent his whole life dreaming of constructing something which would last. In the absence of a town or a cathedral, he plumped for this bridge. You couldn't really expect him to let it be destroyed—not a regular of the old school, sir, not likely! I'm sure he had read the whole of Kipling as a boy and I bet he recited chunks of it as the construction gradually took shape above the water. "Yours is the earth and everything that's in it, and which is more, you'll be a man, my son"—I can just hear him!

'He had a highly developed sense of duty and admired a job well done. He was also fond of action—just as you are, sir, just as we all are. This idiotic worship of action, to which our little typists subscribe as much as our great generals! I'm not sure where it all leads to, when I stop to think about it. I've been thinking about it for the last month, sir. Perhaps that silly old fool was really quite a decent fellow at heart? Perhaps he really had a genuine ideal? An ideal as sacred as our own? Perhaps the same ideal as ours? Perhaps all that hocus-pocus he believed in can be traced back to the same source that provides the impetus which lies behind our own activities? That mysterious atmosphere in which our natural impulses stir us to the point of action. Looking at it like that, perhaps, the "result" may have no meaning at all—it's only the intrinsic quality of the effort that counts. Or else this dreamworld, as far as I can see, is simply a hell afflicted with devilish standards which warp our judgment, lead the way to every form of dishonesty and culminate in a result which is bound to be deplorable. I tell you, sir, I've been thinking about all this for the last month. Here we are, for instance, blundering into this part of the world in order to teach Orientals how to handle plastic so as to destroy trains and blow up bridges. Well . . .'

'Tell me what happened in the end.' Colonel Green quietly broke in. 'Nothing matters, remember, apart from action.'

'Nothing matters apart from action, sir . . . Joyce's expression when he came out of his hide-out! And he didn't falter. He struck home according to the text-book, I'll vouch for that. All he needed was just a little more judgment. The other chap rushed at him with such fury that they both rolled down the slope towards the river. They didn't stop till they were almost in the water. To the naked eye they looked as if they were both lying there quite still. But I saw the details through my glasses. One was on top of the other. The body in uniform was crushing the naked blood-stained body, crushing it with all its weight, while two furious hands were squeezing the other's throat. I could see it all quite clearly. He was stretched out with his arms flung wide, next to the corpse in which the dagger was still embedded. At that moment, sir, he realised his mistake, I'm sure. He realised, I'm sure he realised, that he had misjudged the Colonel.

'I saw him. His hand was close to the hilt of his knife. He seized it. He stiffened. I could almost see his muscles flexing. For a moment I thought he had made up his mind.

But it was too late. He had no strength left. He had given all he had. He was unable to do anything more—or else he was unwilling to. He dropped his knife and gave in. Total surrender, sir. You know what it's like, when you have to give up completely? He resigned himself to his fate. He moved his lips and uttered just one word. No one will ever know if it was an oath or a prayer, or even a polite conventional expression of utter despair. He wasn't bloody-minded, sir, or if he was he didn't show it. He always treated his superior officers with respect. Good God, Shears and I only just managed to stop him springing to attention each time he spoke to either of us! I bet you he said "sir" before passing out, sir. Everything depended on him. It was all over.

'Then several things happened all at once, several "facts," as you would no doubt call them, sir. They were all muddled in my mind, but I've sorted them out since. The train was arriving. The roar of the engine was growing louder every second; but it wasn't loud enough to drown the yells of that lunatic, who was shouting for help at the top of his voice in parade-ground tones!

'There I was, unable to do anything, sir. I couldn't have done better than he did. I certainly couldn't; no one could —except, pehaps, Shears, Shears! It was then that I heard someone else shouting. Shears's voice, that was it. It echoed right round the valley. The voice of a raving madman, sir! I could only make out one word: "Strike!" He too had realised, and sooner than I had. But it was too late now.

'Some time afterwards I saw a man in the water. He was swimming towards the enemy bank. It was him. It was Shears. He too worshipped action, action at any price. A crazy thing to do. He had gone mad, just as I had, as a result of that morning. He didn't have a chance. I felt like dashing out to join him, but it would have taken over two hours to climb down from the O.P.

'He didn't have a dog's chance. He was swimming frantically, but it took him several minutes to get across. And in that time, sir, the train was already on the bridge. the splendid River Kwai bridge which our comrades-in-arms had built! Just then—just then, I remember, I saw a group of Japanese soldiers; they had heard the yells and were stumbling down the slope.

'They were the ones who dealt with Shears as he climbed out of the water. He got rid of two of them. Two thrusts of his knife, sir, I didn't miss a thing. He wasn't going to let himself be captured alive, but a rifle butt came down on the back of his head. He collapsed. Joyce was also on the ground, lying quite still. The Colonel was getting to his feet. The soldiers had cut the wire. There was nothing more we could do, sir.'

'There's always some further action to take,' Colonel Green observed.

'Always some further action to take, sir . . . After that there was an explosion. The train, which no one had thought of stopping, had blown up on the fog-signal I had laid this side of the bridge, just below the O.P. A bit of luck, that! I'd forgotten all about it. The engine came off the track and plunged into the river, bringing two or three coaches down with it. A few men were drowned. A fair amount of stores lost; but the damage could be repaired in a few days—that was the net result. But it caused quite a lot of excitement on the opposite bank.'

'A pretty fine sight, I should think, all the same,' Colonel Green consoled him.

'A very fine sight, sir, for those that like that sort of thing. So I tried to think how I could make it look even finer. I didn't forget the principles of the Force, sir. I really wracked my brains at that moment to see if there was anything more I could do in the way of action.'

'There's always something more to be done in the way of action,' Colonel Green dreamily remarked.

'Always something to be done . . . That must be true, since everyone says so. That was Shears's motto. I remembered it.'

Warden stopped talking for a moment, overcome by this last thought; then went on in a softer tone of voice.

'I thought hard, sir. I thought as hard as I possibly could, while the group of soldiers swarmed round Joyce and

Shears. Shears was certainly still alive, and so perhaps was Joyce, in spite of what that dirty dog had done to him.

'I could see only one possible way of taking action, sir. My two partisans were still in position with the mortar. They could fire just as easily on the group of Japs as on the bridge, and the group was just as easy to hit. I gave them that as their target. I waited a little longer. I saw the soldiers pick up the prisoners and start carrying them off. They were both still alive. It was the worst that could have happened. Colonel Nicholson brought up the rear, hanging his head as though he was deep in thought. I wonder what he was thinking, sir. I suddenly made up my mind, while there was still time.

'I gave the order to fire. The Siamese understood at once. We had trained them pretty thoroughly, sir. It was a splendid fireworks display. Another fine sight for those in the O.P. Close cross-fire. I handled the mortar myself, and I'm not such a bad shot.'

'Good results?' Colonel Green broke in.

'Good results, sir. The first shells burst right among the group. A stroke of luck! Both our chaps were blown to pieces. I confirmed that by looking through my glasses. Believe me, sir, please believe me, I didn't want to leave the job half-done either. All three of them, I should have said. The Colonel as well. There was nothing left of him. Three birds with one stone. Not bad!

'After that? After that, sir, I fired all the shells I had. There were quite a lot. Our hand-grenades as well. The position had been well selected. We sprayed the ground pretty thoroughly. I was a bit overwrought, I admit. The stuff was falling a bit indiscriminately, on the rest of the company rushing out of the camp, on the derailed train, in which everyone was shrieking, and also on the bridge. The two Siamese were as worked up as I was. The Japs fired back. Soon the smoke spread and crept up as far as us, more or less blotting out the valley and the River Kwai. We were cut off in a stinking grey fog. There was no more ammo, nothing else to fire. So we retired.

'Since then I've often thought about that decision of

mine, sir. I'm now convinced I couldn't have done anything else. I took the only line of conduct possible. It was really the only proper action I could have taken.'

'The only proper action,' the Colonel agreed.

THE END

Fontana Paperbacks
Non-fiction

Fontana is a leading paperback publisher of non-fiction. Below are some recent titles.

- ☐ All in a Day's Work *Danny Danziger* £3.50
- ☐ Policeman's Gazette *Harry Cole* £2.95
- ☐ The Caring Trap *Jenny Pulling* £2.95
- ☐ I Fly Out with Bright Feathers *Allegra Taylor* £3.95
- ☐ Managing Change and Making it Stick *Roger Plant* £3.50
- ☐ Staying Vegetarian *Lynne Alexander* £3.95
- ☐ The Aforesaid Child *Clare Sullivan* £2.95
- ☐ A Grain of Truth *Jack Webster* £2.95
- ☐ John Timpson's Early Morning Book *John Timpson* £3.95
- ☐ Negotiate to Close *Gary Karrass* £3.95
- ☐ Re-making Love *Barbara Ehrereich* £3.95
- ☐ Steve McQueen *Penina Spiegel* £3.95
- ☐ A Vet for All Seasons *Hugh Lasgarn* £2.95
- ☐ Holding the Reins *Juliet Solomon* £3.95
- ☐ Another Voice *Auberon Waugh* £3.95
- ☐ Beyond Fear *Dorothy Rowe* £4.95
- ☐ A Dictionary of Twentieth Century Quotations
    Nigel Rees £4.95
- ☐ Another Bloody Tour *Frances Edmonds* £2.50
- ☐ The Book of Literary Lists *Nicholas Parsons* £3.95

You can buy Fontana paperbacks at your local bookshop or newsagent. Or you can order them from Fontana Paperbacks, Cash Sales Department, Box 29, Douglas, Isle of Man. Please send a cheque, postal or money order (not currency) worth the purchase price plus 22p per book for postage (maximum postage required is £3).

NAME (Block letters) _____

ADDRESS _____

_____

_____